"I'm just not the romantic type."

"No?"

"No," she whispered.

Dan leaned his head down to hers as he studied her, his smile so close to her mouth that her parted lips longed to taste it. God, Kinley thought dazedly, when was the last time she'd sat in the gardens with a man who made her toes curl?

Much, much too long ago.

She rested her hands on his shoulders, fingers flexing into the muscles there. "This is not at all like me," she assured him. "And in a few minutes I'm going to leave this bench, go home and attend to some work matters before I get any rest tonight. But first…"

And because this night seemed to have a touch of magic in the air, she covered his rogue's smile with her lips. Just a taste, she promised herself. After the past few hours together, she didn't think he'd mind too badly.

The eager way his arms went around her proved he didn't mind in the least.

Whe

MATCHED BY MOONLIGHT

BY
GINA WILKINS

Published in Great Britain 2014
by Mills & Boon, an imprint of Harlequin (UK) Limited,
Eton House, 18-24 Paradise Road, Richmond, Surrey, TW9 1SR

© 2014 Gina Wilkins

ISBN: 978 0 263 91255 5

23-0114

Harlequin (UK) Limited's policy is to use papers that are natural, renewable and recyclable products and made from wood grown in sustainable forests. The logging and manufacturing processes conform to the legal environmental regulations of the country of origin.

Printed and bound in Spain
by Blackprint CPI, Barcelona

Gina Wilkins is a bestselling and award-winning author who has written more than seventy novels for Mills & Boon. She credits her successful career in romance to her long, happy marriage and her three "extraordinary" children.

A lifelong resident of central Arkansas, Ms Wilkins sold her first book to Mills & Boon in 1987 and has been writing full-time since. She has appeared on the Waldenbooks, B. Dalton and *USA TODAY* bestseller lists. She is a three-time recipient of a Maggie Award for Excellence, sponsored by Georgia Romance Writers, and has won several awards from the reviewers of *RT Book Reviews*.

In special memory of my book-loving mother, a lifelong Harlequin fan. One of her favorite verses was, "I will lift up my eyes unto the hills, from which cometh my strength." She passed along her love of both romance and the mountains to me.

Chapter One

Early-morning fog danced in wispy tendrils outside the bay window of the breakfast nook, making the rural, southwestern Virginia landscape resemble a dreamy watercolor. Leaning against the cherry window frame, Kinley Carmichael sipped cinnamon-laced coffee and studied the pink-and-gray sunrise framed by lace curtains. Her sentimental younger sister, Bonnie, would see that lovely spring view and sigh, thinking of fairy tales and romance. Practical and pragmatic Kinley saw an excellent photo-op for the Bride Mountain Inn website. In fact, maybe tomorrow morning she'd head out early with her camera in hopes of capturing a similar scene for advertising purposes, aiming to appeal to potential guests looking for quiet relaxation in pristine, natural surroundings…just the ambiance the inn aimed to provide.

She almost laughed when the wistful sigh she'd predicted sounded from behind her. "Isn't it beautiful?" Bonnie asked in little more than a whisper, her tone almost reverent. "Even after living here just over two years, I never get tired of seeing that view first thing in the morning."

"That view would make a perfect cover for a marketing brochure. I'm considering going out in the morning with my camera to try to capture it."

Bonnie gave her a teasingly chiding look. "You can't capture magic, Kinley."

"I can try," she answered cheerily. "And then I'll do my best to package and sell it."

Bonnie's second sigh was more resigned than romanticized. With her blond hair, blue eyes and flawless skin, she looked a bit like a porcelain doll and had the perfect, petite figure to match. She wore her favored uniform of a pretty, lace-trimmed top and a gauzy skirt, adding to her vaguely old-world appeal. Her delicate appearance and openly sentimental nature led some people to think she was meek and easily pushed around. Those people were wrong. Behind that sweet face was a sharp mind and a fierce resolve that both her siblings could attest to. Though she was the youngest, it was wholly due to Bonnie's determination and insistence that the three of them were now running the bed-and-breakfast together.

As close as they were, the two sisters had always been very different in nature. Even their choice of clothing illustrated those dissimilarities, Kinley thought fondly. In contrast to Bonnie's soft, floaty garments, Kinley wore gray slacks with a gray-and-white shell and a pearl-gray three-quarter-sleeve cardigan suitable for the cool spring morning. Bonnie had once accused her of dressing as if she were always expecting an impromptu business meeting, and Kinley supposed that was accurate enough. But her tailored style suited her just fine.

Peering out the window again, Bonnie nodded toward a particularly foggy patch in the garden, near the tall, graceful fountain. "Look at the way the fog swirls just there, almost as if it's alive. Do you think if you set your camera on a tripod and used a very slow lens speed, you'd catch a peek of the bride hiding in the mist?"

Kinley glanced automatically toward the open kitchen doorway, making sure no guests had overheard her sister's fanciful speculation. "Don't even joke about that. You know how I feel about that old legend being connected to the inn."

"You have no whimsy, Kinley."

"So you keep saying." The mostly-forgotten legend had long been a sore spot between them. During the past hundred years or so, there had been a few reported sightings on Bride Mountain of a ghostly woman dressed all in white who appeared in the mist to newly engaged couples. An old local story speculated that those who were lucky enough to spot the bride were meant to live happily ever after. Bonnie had initially suggested that reviving the legend could be a charming way to promote the wedding services they offered at Bride Mountain Inn. Kinley and their cynical older brother, Logan, had firmly vetoed that idea, both wary of the clientele who would potentially be attracted to their inn by a ghost story.

Bonnie shrugged. "You can believe what you want. I still like to think that Uncle Leo and Aunt Helen really did see the bride on the night he proposed to her in the garden."

Kinley shook her head indulgently. "Uncle Leo just loved seeing your reaction to that story every time he told it to you. You were always his favorite," she added without resentment.

Bonnie had fallen in love with the inn as a child when their mother had brought them for frequent visits with their great-uncle Leo Finley, the second-generation owner of the place. Kinley had been eleven years old, Logan twelve and Bonnie only eight when Leo's beloved wife, their great-aunt Helen, had died following a brief illness. Afterward, Leo had closed the bed-and-breakfast, having lost the heart to keep it open, though he hadn't been willing to sell it, either. He'd lived alone in the former inn for the next eighteen years, doing basic maintenance but letting the place run down a bit as both he and the building had grown older. When he'd died two and a half years ago, he'd left it all equally to his only surviving family, his late niece's three now-grown children.

Bonnie had dreamed almost all her life of reopening the inn, and had even majored in hotel management in college as preparation. She had begged, cajoled and bullied her older siblings into joining her in this undertaking when the property became theirs—and because both Kinley and Logan had been at crossroads in their lives at that time, they had allowed themselves to be persuaded.

Still the compulsive overachiever she'd always been, Kinley was as determined as her sister to make a success of the venture. For her, the inn was a test of her competence, her business acumen. A practical use for her business and real-estate degrees, and a way to boost her confidence that had been bruised in a painful divorce. A fresh start, a new challenge, a new life. For Logan, it was just a job, a way to pay the bills and still be his own boss. For Bonnie, it was simply what made her happy.

Opening one of the two large ovens in the top-of-the-line kitchen, Bonnie drew out a delicious-smelling breakfast casserole. She'd assembled two of the large dishes last night and had only needed to pop them in the oven this morning. She would serve them with sliced fruit and the bran muffins now browning in the second oven. Yogurt and cold cereals were also available upon request. Bonnie loved spoiling their guests.

Kinley glanced at her watch. Breakfast would be served in the adjoining dining room at seven, just a few minutes away. "I'll help you set up."

Bonnie sent a smile over her shoulder as she carried the casserole dish into the other room. "Thanks. Rhoda seems to be running a little late this morning."

"What else is new?" Kinley muttered under her breath, loading a tray with serving dishes. Helping with breakfast service was not on her tightly arranged agenda for the day, but she had a little extra time built in for flexibility. Her siblings teased her often about trying to schedule unexpected developments.

She and Bonnie were both fond of Rhoda Foley, the full-time housekeeper who had worked for them since they'd reopened the inn, but their employee definitely marched to her own drummer—not to mention her own clock. Rhoda was a hard worker, tackling everything from cleaning to decorating to helping with meal service, as needed, but she was a little quirky, to say the least. "You need to talk with her again, Bonnie. We have the Sossaman-Thompson wedding this weekend, and everything must run smoothly. You're going to need Rhoda's help. And that travel writer, Dan Phelan, is coming tomorrow. It's important that everything has to look perfect while he's here. We could get a ton of bookings from his article in *Modern South* magazine, assuming he enjoys his time here as much as we hope he does, of course."

Bonnie chuckled. "Of course. Piece of cake."

Placing the food in silver-plated chafing dishes on the antique serving sideboard, Kinley looked around in satisfaction at the airy dining room decorated in traditional Southern style. Rather than one long, stuffy table, they'd utilized four round tables in the big room, each seating six. Silver candlesticks, snowy linens and fragrant flowers in crystal vases decorated the tables, which sat on an antique carpet and were illuminated by an antique silver-plate and crystal chandelier salvaged from an old Virginia plantation house. The chandelier had hung in this room since her great-grandfather built the inn, though Bonnie had it refurbished when they'd restored the place for reopening.

Despite the formal touches, the room was cozy, warm, welcoming. As was the rest of the inn that had been lovingly and painstakingly restored before they'd officially opened for business just over a year ago.

"How could he not write a positive review?" Kinley smiled fondly at her sister. "Every inch of the inn is beautiful, the service is superb, the setting idyllic. There's nothing negative to write. Almost all thanks to you, by the way. I plan to impress the old guy with my business facts and figures, you'll charm the bow tie off him and Logan…well, maybe Logan should just work quietly in the background," she added with a wry laugh.

Stepping back to eye the sideboard with a thoroughly appraising glance, Bonnie asked absently, "What makes you think he's an easily-charmed old man with a bow tie?"

"I have no idea what he's like. I'm just teasing." Kinley moved out of the way when the first group of four guests wandered in, a young couple who were checking out the inn as a potential site for their wedding in the fall and the bride-to-be's mother and sister. Kinley had a meeting scheduled with them later that day, so she simply bade them good morning and left them to enjoy their breakfast. They were followed in not long afterward by Lon and Jan Mayberry, a blissful pair of honeymooners in their late forties, and by Travis Cross and Gordon Monroe, a pleasant couple enjoying a long-weekend escape from their stressful jobs in Richmond. A nice group, Kinley thought. She always enjoyed visiting with friendly guests of the inn, though Bonnie usually got to know them better than she did.

Two hours later she helped her sister clear away the remains of the breakfast buffet. Rhoda had still not made an appearance, nor had she answered her cell phone when Bonnie tried to call. They were going to get serious about trying to find her if she didn't show up soon. Rhoda's timing wasn't exactly dependable, but she never just skipped a day at work without at least calling. Bonnie said she would drive to Rhoda's house if she still hadn't shown up by nine-thirty.

The last of the breakfast diners lingered over coffee at their tables, discussing plans for the day in low voices, admiring the gardens visible through the big dining-room windows, looking full and content. Four of the seven guest suites were occupied on this Thursday morning and all but one of the rooms were booked for the weekend, counting the one the travel writer had reserved. The Sossaman wedding would take place Saturday afternoon and the bride and groom had agreed to allow the writer to include photos from the ceremony in his article. The weather prediction was for a nice, clear day. Forsythia, irises, tulips, creeping phlox and early-blooming roses had thrived in the nice temperatures of the past couple of weeks in May, adding splashes of vivid color to the bright green leaves on the trees surrounding the wedding gazebo in the back garden.

Everything was perfect, she assured herself, refilling her coffee cup and taking a bracing sip. Or at least as perfect as she and her siblings could make it appear to be in front of their guests—one travel writer, in particular.

Lost in her fantasy of a glowing write-up followed by a flood of bookings and accolades, she jumped dramatically when a loud, jarring crash came from the front of the inn. A couple of guests gasped, and one gave a startled little screech. Hot coffee splashed over the rim of Kinley's cup. She hissed a curse, quickly setting down the cup and shaking her stinging hand. She was running toward the front of the inn before the sound of the crash fully faded away.

Grimacing, she threw open the front door and viewed the scene outside as Bonnie groaned behind her in despair.

An old pickup truck had slammed into the front post of the portico that jutted out from the front of the inn to provide cover for unloading cars at the front door. The post had splintered in half and now that whole corner of the shingled portico sagged dangerously downward. The top half of the post, along with some small debris, had landed on the now badly dented pickup.

Rhoda climbed out of the driver's seat of the truck, shoving a broken piece of gingerbread trim out of the way. Her curly salt-and-pepper hair was wildly disheveled around her plain face, but she looked uninjured, to Kinley's relief.

"I'm so sorry," Rhoda called out the minute she was clear of her wrecked truck. "I overslept and I'd forgotten to charge my phone so I couldn't call you. I stupidly glanced at my watch just as I started to drive under the portico and I misjudged the turn. I'm okay, but I'm so sorry. I have insurance. It will cover the damage, of course."

Reaching the older woman first, Kinley caught her nervously flailing hands in a calming grip. "You're sure you're all right? Should we take you to be checked out? I can drive or we can call an ambulance."

Rhoda shook her head vehemently. "No, I'm fine. Really. I was wearing my seat belt and I wasn't going very fast. The truck's too old for an air bag, so at least I didn't get hit in the face with one of those. Just got a fright when it hit, that's all."

"You're lucky the whole portico didn't come down on you."

"I know."

"Hey! Everyone get back." Logan came running around one corner of the inn, waving an arm to punctuate his order to the gawkers now gathered in the open doorway. "No one should stand under the portico until I make sure it's fully supported again. Bonnie, lock the front door and have your guests use the side entrance for now."

"I'm so sorry, Logan." Rhoda pulled her hands from Kinley's comforting grasp and began to twist them in front of her. "I'll move my truck."

"No." Stopping nearby, Logan pushed a hand through his slightly shaggy brown hair as he surveyed the damage with a frown. "Let me handle it."

Having obligingly moved out from under the portico, Kinley turned to look again, wincing at the sight. It could have been much worse, she assured herself. At least only one post was broken, so the whole portico hadn't come down. But still, it looked sad sagging that way, some of the delicate gingerbread trim dangling precariously.

"We have a wedding Saturday," she reminded her brother. "Rehearsal is tomorrow evening."

He nodded. "I'll put in a call to Hank Charles. I'm pretty sure he made an extra post when we commissioned him to craft these, just so he'd have the pattern if he needed it again. If he still has it, we'll get it delivered and installed as quickly as possible."

Kinley put a hand to her head with a sudden groan. "That travel writer is due tomorrow morning. He's going to be taking photographs of the inn. I don't suppose there's any way...?"

"Oh, hon, I'm so sorry," Rhoda moaned again.

His unshaven jaw clenching, Logan nodded shortly. "I'll do what I can."

A black car came up the drive and stopped in the guest parking area. Wondering who would be arriving this early on a Thursday, Kinley glanced that way. A tall, dark-haired man who appeared to be in his early thirties—and in excellent physical condition, she couldn't help noting—climbed out of the driver's seat and paused to study the commotion around the front of the inn. She didn't recognize him. He was dressed casually in somewhat rumpled khakis and a dark green cotton shirt with the cuffs rolled back at the wrists. He didn't look like a salesman, nor a traveler looking for a room. After a moment, he moved toward them.

As harried as she was by Rhoda's accident and the resulting mess, Kinley was startled by the instant jolt of pulse-tripping physical awareness that shot through her when the newcomer smiled at her. She'd have thought she'd be too distracted to be dumbfounded by a sexy grin, but apparently her recently dormant feminine instincts were still alive and healthy. Shoving those ill-timed responses to the back of her mind, she pasted on as professional an expression as possible under the circumstances and greeted him. "May I help you?"

He met her eyes, and she noted that his were very blue, intriguingly so in contrast with his longish dark hair and tanned skin. Wow. She had to force herself to resist automatically checking his ring finger. When he spoke, it was in a pleasantly deep voice that only strengthened her immediate attraction to him. "Are you Kinley Carmichael?"

Even the way he said her name gave her a little thrill. How odd. "Yes, I am. What can I do for you?"

Something about his sweeping glance before he answered made her self-conscious—but not in a bad way. The hint of reciprocated approval in this great-looking guy's expression was a nice little boost to her ego.

His smile deepened, pushing a slash of delicious dimples into his tanned cheeks. "I'm Dan Phelan. I know you didn't expect me until tomorrow, but I found myself ahead of schedule. I—ah—hope I didn't arrive at an inconvenient time."

Kinley felt her heart sink abruptly. The quick flush of pleasure changed abruptly to dismay. The travel writer hadn't been scheduled to arrive until tomorrow. She had wanted everything to be so perfect when he arrived. Why had he shown up at just this inopportune moment?

It was only nine o'clock, she thought in silent despair. What more could possibly go wrong today?

Though she immediately schooled her expression, it was apparent to Dan that Kinley Carmichael had recognized his name, and that she hadn't been happy to hear it. Considering he'd obviously shown up in the middle of a crisis, he couldn't blame her, but he had to admit it piqued his pride to have an attractive woman appear so distressed by meeting him.

He wouldn't have labeled Kinley a classic beauty, but he liked the look of her oval face framed by an angular, gold-streaked brown bob, gray-blue eyes that met his with a directness he found refreshing and a mouth with a full lower lip that could only be described as kissable. She was on the tallish side, maybe five-eight, with long legs and a slender figure more aptly defined as athletic than voluptuous. Just his type—though the way her eyes had darkened when he introduced himself was hardly an auspicious beginning.

A fiftysomething woman in a peasant top, faded jeans and sandals, her wildly curling hair more gray than dark, looked from Kinley to Dan and then gasped in sudden comprehension. "You're not the travel writer, are you? The one who's supposed to come tomorrow?"

He nodded. "My itinerary changed unexpectedly. If there's no room available for me here tonight, I'll stay somewhere nearby and come back tomorrow."

Her smile firmly in place again, Kinley spoke up. "Of course we have a room for you, Mr. Phelan. We're delighted to have you."

He had to admire the warmth she managed to inject into the welcome despite the dismay he'd seen pass fleetingly through her eyes. Though it had caught her off guard when he'd shown up a day early, his first impression of Kinley was that she was not easily rattled.

"Please, call me Dan." He glanced again at the damaged truck and portico. "I seem to have arrived at a bad time."

"It's my fault," the older woman said firmly. "I hit the post. The inn is usually immaculate. Beautiful. The Carmichaels run a first-class operation. Don't you dare write a bad review because of my negligence!"

The way she shook her finger at him reminded him of his favorite childhood nanny, Adele. She'd had a way of making her displeasure known with just a judicious wave of that slightly bent finger. Of all the string of nannies his generally disengaged parents had hired to look after him, Adele was the only one he recalled very clearly. That memory made him smile as he murmured, "I wouldn't dream of it."

Kinley placed a hand on the woman's shoulder and Dan saw her give a little squeeze. "It was an accident, Rhoda. No one is blaming you. We're all relieved that you weren't hurt. Dan, this is Rhoda Foley, who works with us here at the inn."

Despite the awkward circumstances, Kinley made it clear that she was standing by her employee. Dan saw no evidence of irritation with the older woman, merely a matter-of-fact acceptance and what seemed to be genuine concern for her well-being. Nor did he think Kinley's kindness was put on for his benefit. Rhoda's fierce loyalty to her employers was apparent. His positive first impression of Kinley bumped up another notch.

"It's very nice to meet you, Ms. Foley."

She mumbled a reply, though she continued to shoot looks of warning at him.

Kinley cleared her throat. "Rhoda, why don't you go inside and have a cup of tea to calm your nerves while Logan takes care of your truck?"

Having sent the older woman on her way, she turned back to the men. "Dan, this is my brother, Logan Carmichael."

Though he saw the family resemblance as they briefly shook hands, Dan noted that Logan's features were more roughly carved than his sister's, his jaw squared beneath a three-day growth of dark beard. His brown hair was a shade darker than Kinley's, and his eyes were hazel, shadowed with what appeared to be a permanent frown. Maybe it was just the damage to the inn that made him look so stern, but Dan suspected Kinley's brother wasn't the lighthearted type even under the best of circumstances.

A petite blonde with a sweet face and angelic smile came out the side door of the inn and approached them. "I've got Rhoda settled down in the kitchen with some tea. Logan, do you need me to make any calls for you?"

Logan shrugged. "I'll get the guys to help me start the repairs right away. You can deal with the insurance."

"Dan, this is our sister, Bonnie," Kinley said. "Bonnie, meet Dan Phelan, the writer for *Modern South* magazine. He's going to be spending an extra day with us. Isn't that nice?"

Dan couldn't help but be amused by Kinley's too-cheery tone. Though she was doing her best to hide it, he would bet she thought it was anything but nice that he'd shown up twenty-four hours early.

If Bonnie was as displeased as her sister, it wasn't evident in her pleasant expression. She bore only a faint resemblance to her siblings, her eyes a deep blue, her coloring fair, her stature more compact. *Striking* had been the first adjective to pop into his mind with Kinley. He would have described Bonnie as pretty. Yet his attention continued to be focused primarily on Kinley, even as Bonnie spoke to him. "Rhoda told me you were here. It's a pleasure to meet you, Mr. Phelan. Welcome to our inn."

"It's Dan. And thank you. It's a beautiful place."

He wasn't just being polite. Despite the current minor damage, the inn really was lovely. The multi-bayed Queen Anne–style building was surrounded by an inviting wraparound porch that opened onto the drive-through portico. The siding was a pale gray, the trim pristine white. The front door was painted a bright red and featured leaded-glass inserts and sidelights. A stained glass half-round window above the now-sagging portico drew the eye upward to the peaked, shingled roof against the bright blue sky. Colorful spring flowers bloomed in several tidy beds, and the Blue Ridge Mountains, draped in rapidly dissipating morning fog, formed a spectacular backdrop for it all. Compared to those distant peaks, Bride Mountain was little more than a foothill, but the view was breathtaking.

Bonnie motioned apologetically toward the broken

post. "As you can see, we've had a little mishap this morning, but fortunately no one was injured and my brother will see that it's quickly repaired. Please come in through the side door. Breakfast service ended at nine, but I'm sure I can find something for you if you're hungry."

"I've eaten already, thank you."

"Coffee, then?"

"Sounds good. I'll just get my bags."

"Um—let me get them for you," Logan offered, not doing a particularly good job of hiding his reluctance.

Because he'd seen Kinley give her brother a sharp nudge, Dan fought a grin as he declined politely. "I'll let you get to your repairs. I'll carry my own bags. I pack light."

Nodding rather curtly, Logan turned back to the damaged portico, already lifting his cell phone to his ear to summon assistance.

"I'll help you bring in your things," Kinley offered, subtly directing Dan away from the portico damage and leaving her brother to deal with it. "I'll show you up to your room and then give you the grand tour when you're ready."

"I'd like that," he said, his gaze focused on her face.

She paused a moment, her head slightly tilted as she met his eyes, and he wondered if she had sensed his immediate attraction to her. But she merely smiled and nodded, speaking in the same briskly professional voice she'd used before. "Let's get your bags, and I'll take you in through the side door."

The disarray outside could not be in starker contrast to the tidy inside of Bride Mountain Inn. The side door opened into the dining area rather than the front foyer.

As he followed Kinley through the big room, Dan's gaze was drawn to the large, sparklingly clean back windows that overlooked the gardens and the distant mountains. The room was airy, immaculate and immediately welcoming. It was easy to imagine himself lingering over coffee at one of the round tables and watching the sky brighten over the flowers, fountain and charming Queen Anne gazebo behind the inn.

She led him into the entryway that would have been his first sight of the place had he come in the front door. The matching leaded-glass sidelights on either side of the door flooded the wood-floored foyer with morning sunlight. A small antique reception desk held a big bouquet of fresh flowers, and an old-fashioned mail cubby on the papered wall behind the desk reinforced the old-world-inn feel to the place. Sparkling crystals dangled from the chandelier that lit the two-story space, and a curving, wood-banistered stairway led upstairs.

"Very nice," he commented.

Kinley's quick grin looked more natural than the professional smiles she'd forced after he'd identified himself to her. His initial attraction to her doubled in response. He reminded himself that he was here for business reasons, that he tried to remain objective about the subjects of his articles despite his generally laid-back approach to his job. He hadn't gotten much sleep last night. The past couple of weeks had been stressful. Maybe he was just tired, and a little too susceptible at the moment to a pretty face and an approving smile. He needed a strong cup of coffee, a brisk walk and maybe a nap, after which he was sure he'd have himself under better control.

After plucking a key from behind the desk, Kinley moved toward the stairs. "This way," she said and started up, his computer bag slung over her shoulder.

Carrying a small suitcase in his right hand and a garment bag in the other, he followed. Despite his best efforts, his gaze lingered on the slight sway of her slender hips as she preceded him. He'd always had a thing for slim hips and long legs...

Shaking his head in self-reproach, he made himself raise his eyes. Maybe he'd have two cups of strong coffee, followed by a very long walk to clear his mind. He could just hear his managing editor—who also happened to be his cousin—lecturing him that lusting after his hostess was no way to start an assignment.

Kinley unlocked the third door on the right at the top of the stairs and escorted him inside. The suite was as immaculate as he had come to expect of this place. The furniture was dark wood in Colonial style, the linens pale yellow trimmed in rich cream. A writing desk, flat-screen television, comfortable-looking chair and ottoman, and a minifridge were among the amenities. A small but luxurious private bathroom was stocked with high-end toiletries and supplies. More fresh flowers in a crystal vase adorned the nightstand, along with a bowl of fresh fruit. The view was spectacular. The last traces of fog had burned off, though he thought he glimpsed a lingering wisp near the large fountain that highlighted the flower garden.

He set his bags on the floor near the Colonial dresser. "I have to say the inn is really beautiful."

He was rewarded by another of Kinley's bright smiles. "Thank you. My sister loves decorating and took charge of most of the restoration before we reopened eighteen months ago. Most of what you see is her work."

Reaching out to take his computer bag from her, he nodded toward her as he set the bag on the desk. "And what do *you* love to do?"

She answered without hesitation. "I like the business side of running the inn. The marketing, events planning, bookings, that sort of thing. It's a challenge, and I've always enjoyed a challenge."

"So do I," he murmured without looking away from her. The enthusiasm in her eyes when she talked of her work made him wonder what other passions excited her. After all, he was a healthy, straight, definitely single male.

As if she'd somehow gotten an inkling of the direction his wayward thoughts had taken, her left eyebrow rose a fraction of an inch. She studied him for a moment with a heightened awareness in her expression— not nerves, he decided, but a hint of intrigue. At least, he thought he was reading her correctly.

He cleared his throat. "You said something about coffee?"

It was much too early for anything stronger. He could only hope a strong shot of caffeine would clear his uncharacteristically cloudy head.

Kinley nodded and moved toward the door. "Join me in the dining room whenever you're ready. We'll have coffee, then take that tour I promised."

"I'll be right down." Maybe he'd splash a little cold water on his face first.

"Where is he?" Bonnie asked in an exaggerated whisper as soon as Kinley came downstairs. She had found her sister lurking in the foyer, presumably ready to duck out of sight into the kitchen if Dan had accompanied Kinley down. None of the other guests were around at the moment.

Keeping her own voice low, Kinley replied, "He'll be down in a few minutes for coffee and a tour. Fresh coffee ready?"

Bonnie nodded. "I warmed some of the leftover breakfast pastries, too, in case he wants a snack."

Kinley gave her a thumbs-up sign of approval.

"Can you believe he showed up this morning, of all days?" Bonnie shook her head in dismay. "He couldn't have timed his arrival more inconveniently if he'd tried."

"No kidding," Kinley murmured with a grimace. "A broken post and a sagging portico is hardly the first impression I wanted him to get of the inn. Not to mention that I'm going to have to rearrange my whole schedule now to work him into it today."

"Logan promised it wouldn't take long to fix the front. He said most of it would be done by the end of today, by noon tomorrow for sure."

Kinley focused on the smartphone in her hand, on which she was busily making notes and rearranging scheduled time blocks. "I hope he's right."

Bonnie looked toward the staircase again. "You couldn't have been more wrong in predicting what the travel writer would look like, by the way. He's, like, the opposite of an older man in a bow tie."

Without looking up from her phone, Kinley gave a short laugh. "Yeah, I noticed."

Bonnie flashed a grin. "I thought you might have. He certainly seemed to notice you."

Remembering that moment when her eyes had met

Dan's upstairs, Kinley cleared her throat. Okay, so maybe there'd been a moment of awareness. For a couple of heartbeats, she'd been tempted to give him a sultry smile, toss her hair, maybe flutter her lashes a bit—the standard signs that a woman was interested. Or at least, as best she could remember. It had been so long since she'd flirted with anyone that she wasn't entirely sure she still knew how. She had let the opportunity pass, both because it would have been totally unprofessional of her to flirt with a guest of the inn, and because of her vested interest in the review he would write.

Before she could respond to her sister's teasing, a noise from the stairway alerted her that the subject of their conversation was on his way down. She gave Bonnie a quick look of warning, then turned with a bright smile to greet Dan as he joined them. She'd hoped a few minutes away from him would have gotten her past that initial jolt of attraction, but seeing him bounding lightly down the stairs made her breath catch again. Something about this good-looking guy just got to her in a way no one else had in—well, longer than she could remember.

He carried a small black bag that probably held a camera, reminding her of why he was here. She mentally crossed her fingers that the noises drifting in from outside meant her brother was already busily restoring the front of the inn. Surely Dan would be content to take shots of the other areas of the inn until the front was picture-perfect again.

Sliding her phone into her pocket, she motioned toward the dining room. "Bonnie just told me she has a fresh pot of coffee and some pastries set out for us."

He nodded. "Sounds great."

As she accompanied him and her sister into the other

room, Kinley smiled somewhat smugly. Bonnie's pastries were locally renowned, one frequent guest going so far as to term them "heaven on a plate." Dan already seemed impressed by his suite. After tasting her sister's coffee and pastries, followed by a carefully guided tour of the place, he would undoubtedly be convinced that the inn deserved a glowing write-up.

From this point on, she was going to make sure his only impressions were positive ones. Just as she would make sure to keep her unexpected attraction to him under firm control. She'd had much more luck with business than with romance in the past, and she would do well to keep that in mind when it came to her dealings with this sexy writer.

Chapter Two

Kinley and Dan had just been seated at a window table with their coffee and a plate of pastries when a tall, broad-shouldered woman barged through the side door, followed by a younger, smaller woman and a preschool-age boy. With a slight wince, Kinley recognized the older woman as Eva Sossaman, the mother of the weekend's bride-to-be, Serena Sossaman, who looked embarrassed as she trailed after her fuming mom.

"There you are." Eva pointed a finger accusingly at Kinley. "I need to lodge a complaint about the condition of the inn."

Of course she did. All too aware of Dan sitting there watching, Kinley rose to deal with the notoriously difficult client. Maybe she'd jinxed herself when she'd wondered what else could go wrong today. Considering how many hours remained until bedtime, she didn't even want to think about the answer to that mental question.

She called on all her professional training to greet the indignant client with a cheery smile. "Good morning, Eva. And Serena. What can we do for you?"

"We came to take some photographs for Serena's wedding book," Eva replied firmly. In all Kinley's meetings with them since booking the wedding several months earlier, Eva had almost always been the one to speak up while Serena had pretty much acquiesced to her mother's wishes. "We just saw the front of the inn and we are appalled. Surely you don't expect our guests to be greeted by that mess outside."

"There was a small accident this morning, but my brother is working on repairs now," Kinley assured her. "He promised me that everything will be in place for the wedding. Your guests won't even know what happened by the time they arrive Saturday."

"I hope you're right," Eva snapped. "We've told everyone that the wedding venue is worthy of Serena's wedding and I would hate to be proven wrong."

"You won't be," Bonnie said, moving to stand closer to Kinley. "Everything is absolutely on track for the wedding and our brother will make sure the grounds are ready. Even the weather forecasts are perfect, which is always a gamble this time of year. Serena's wedding is going to be beautiful."

"Ladies, I'd like to introduce you to Dan Phelan," Kinley said before Eva could voice any more complaints. "Dan is the writer for *Modern South* who contacted you about observing your wedding, Serena. Dan, this is our bride-to-be, Serena Sossaman and her mother, Eva."

Eva's scowl transformed immediately into a beaming smile, as Kinley had hoped it might. Barely giving

Serena a chance to murmur a nice-to-meet-you, she nudged her daughter aside and offered her right hand to Dan in a regal gesture. "It's a pleasure to meet you, Mr. Phelan. We're delighted to have you as a guest at my daughter's wedding. I know you'll write a lovely story about it. We've worked very hard for the past year planning every detail."

Dan shook her hand only long enough for civility, though his tone was cordial enough. "I'm sure the wedding will be beautiful. But you should understand that I'm here to write about the inn and other local attractions, and why future couples would want to book events here. I'll use your daughter's wedding only as an example of the services offered here."

A loud thump from the table made everyone turn instinctively to look. Eva's almost-five-year-old grandson had helped himself to a pastry from the plate and was cramming it enthusiastically into his mouth, scattering crumbs and smearing glaze across his face. Added to the stress of the preparations for the rapidly approaching wedding, Eva was babysitting her grandson while his travel-agent parents were away on a business trip. Kinley had been assured by Eva that the trip had been unavoidable, but Serena's brother and sister-in-law had promised to be back the day before the wedding. Eva sighed loudly. "Grayson, you know you're supposed to ask Grandmother before you touch anything."

The boy glanced at her, but didn't slow down on his munching. Eva turned back to Dan. "Grayson is my son's child. He is going to be the ring bearer, aren't you, darling?"

"I'm thirsty," the boy said around a mouthful of soggy pastry.

"I'll get you a glass of milk," Bonnie offered, pulling out a chair for him and offering him a napkin. "Eva, Serena, can I get you some coffee? Or iced tea, perhaps? Feel free to help yourself to a pastry, if you like."

Taking advantage of the opportunity to escape, Kinley spoke to Dan. "Why don't I show you around while Bonnie chats with Serena and her mother? If you ladies will excuse us."

Without giving Eva a chance to detain them longer, Kinley took Dan's arm to rush him out of the dining room and into the foyer.

He smiled knowingly at her when they were alone. "A challenging customer, huh?"

Because she would never gossip about a customer, Kinley merely smiled. "We do our best to satisfy even the most exacting client. I'm sure Serena and her mother will be very happy with the services we'll provide for the wedding Saturday. Now, shall we begin our tour? I thought we'd start inside and then view the gardens."

Taking her cue to change the subject, Dan slipped into a professional manner that matched hers. He removed a small camera from the bag he slung over his shoulder by a thin strap. "Maybe you'd like to stand beside the reception desk? I want to take some preliminary photos during our tour. I'll try to capture the welcoming atmosphere of this foyer. That chandelier is great, by the way."

Kinley automatically straightened her cardigan as she moved to the desk. Though she hadn't been prepared specifically for photos today, she felt somewhat vindicated in her style choices by knowing her outfit was quite appropriate for a magazine shot. Maybe she'd have added a bit more color had she known, but this would do.

"The chandelier is original to the inn," she said. "As is the desk."

Dan was already focusing on her, his gaze fixed on the camera screen. She didn't see how he was going to get the chandelier in that shot, but maybe he just wanted a close-up of her and the desk this time.

"I read the history of the inn you emailed me," he commented absently, still looking at her image on the screen. "Built by your great-grandfather in the mid-1930s. He and his wife ran it until their son, Leo Finley, eventually took it over. Leo kept the inn open until his wife died some twenty years ago, after which it was closed until you and your brother and sister inherited the place."

She smiled in approval. "You did read the history."

After snapping a couple more shots, he looked up from the camera. "I try to be prepared."

She nodded. "That's my motto, too."

He chuckled. "Why does that not surprise me?"

They grinned at each other in a moment of silent communication that felt oddly like bonding—as if they already knew each other, in a way, even though they'd met only an hour or so earlier. Brushing off such uncharacteristic foolishness, she stepped away from the desk and motioned toward the staircase as she went back into her tour-guide spiel. "We have five suites upstairs, the other four very similar to yours. Two handicap-accessible suites are on this main floor. We aren't set up for children, so we accept only guests over the age of twelve. We direct callers with younger children to several local motels that are more family oriented."

"A nice little perk for your guests who want to get away from kids," he murmured.

She nodded and continued, "Bonnie lives full-time downstairs in the basement apartment. It's accessible only from the outside, to keep it separate from the inn. Uncle Leo converted it into living quarters for himself and his wife many years ago, and that was where he continued to live even after he closed the inn. We had it renovated for Bonnie's use. We use the attic for storage."

"You don't live here?"

Leading him toward the common parlor, she shook her head. "I spend the night downstairs occasionally, especially when we want to get an early start the next day, but I rent a house nearby."

"And your brother?"

"Logan lives in the caretaker's cottage at the back of the property, just down the hillside from the gazebo."

Dan nodded thoughtfully. "So you all work together but you've managed to maintain private residences. Good idea."

She smiled over her shoulder before entering the room they called the parlor. "We know that even the closest of siblings should give each other plenty of space, especially if they want to remain close."

"I don't have any siblings, myself, but that sounds like a reasonable philosophy."

"We think so." Entering the parlor, she greeted the couple who sat on one of the comfortable sofas, both studying the screen of a tablet computer one of them held. They looked up when she and Dan came into the room. "Dan, this is Travis Cross and Gordon Monroe, who are visiting us for a few days. Guys, meet Dan Phelan, a travel writer who's staying in room 203."

After exchanging polite greetings, Gordon explained, "Travis and I were just looking at a list of nearby attractions, trying to decide how to spend the day. We're thinking about driving down to Wytheville and checking out a few of the museums."

"Good choice," Kinley assured them. The inn was located close to the Blacksburg-Christiansburg-Radford area, bordered by the Blue Ridge Mountains on the south and the Allegheny Mountains to the north. Historic Wytheville was less than an hour's drive south. She would be sure and encourage Dan to mention the many local attractions in his article.

Travis and Gordon obligingly posed in conversation with Kinley for Dan to snap a few photos of the common room in use. Dan thanked them for their cooperation, but Kinley could tell the couple rather liked the idea of appearing in the magazine. Dan chose several angles to maximize the view of the room Bonnie had decorated in inviting Southern style. Kinley considered igniting the gas logs for the photos, but decided to leave it alone for now. Maybe they would take more photos in here before he left, perhaps with a crackling fire in the background.

Two games tables were positioned at the far side of the room, and an eclectic assortment of games were displayed on nearby shelves. As Travis and Gordon departed for their museum outing, Kinley explained to Dan that almost every evening guests gathered around those tables for games and socializing. "They tell us it's nice to simply unplug their electronics for a few hours and play some old-fashioned board games, face-to-face with other people."

"I'd like to get a shot of your guests playing the

games, if no one objects. I happen to like game nights myself."

That didn't particularly surprise her. Dan seemed like the social type. That was probably a benefit to him in his travel-writing job, making it easy for him to draw out his interview subjects. Not that he'd had to resort to that talent with her. She'd had her sales spiel ready from the moment she'd received notice that the inn would be featured in the magazine.

Continuing in that vein, she motioned toward the doorway. "Ready to see the grounds?"

"Absolutely," he assured her with a smile that almost made her forget her practiced presentation.

Okay, so she hadn't expected the writer to be quite this interesting on his own. Hadn't been prepared to get so lost in his vivid blue eyes that she had to pause for a moment to remember which way to turn upon leaving the parlor. Could not have predicted that her skin would warm and her breath would hitch a bit when he reached around her to open the back door, his arm brushing her shoulder with the gesture. It was so very rare that anyone managed to sidetrack her that she wasn't quite sure how to process that.

Dan was obligingly attentive as Kinley led him along the paths through the gardens. She pointed out the invitingly placed swings and benches and the secluded, nicely shaded nook that would eventually be called the Meditation Garden, which would incorporate a koi pond and perhaps a couple of nice sculpture pieces. Beyond that section was the starting point for a moderately challenging hiking trail through the woods to the peak of

Bride Mountain and then around to the bottom and back up to the inn, just over six miles start to finish.

He snapped a photo of the trailhead sign. "I suppose you've made that hike a few times."

She chuckled. "I could just about walk it blindfolded by now. My brother and sister and I used to love hiking the trail when we visited here as kids."

Lowering his camera, he turned back to her, studying her face as he leaned one shoulder against an oak tree trunk in a casually comfortable pose that suited his easy tone. "The inn was closed during most of your childhood, wasn't it? Do you remember it being open to guests?"

She glanced toward the back of the inn. A row of wooden rockers lined the long back porch. Only the honeymooners sat there now, rocking, sipping tea, chatting and watching Kinley give the tour. She could almost picture her younger self and her late mom sitting there rocking and drinking lemonade and enjoying the sounds of a lazy summer afternoon while Logan tagged behind Leo doing maintenance chores and Bonnie played innkeeper with her dolls. The image was bittersweet, making her smile even as her heart ached with missing her mother.

"I was eleven when my great-uncle closed the place after my great-aunt died, so I have some vague recollections of it being open to guests."

"Do you remember your great-aunt well?"

"Yes. She was a very sweet woman. Uncle Leo adored her. He never fully recovered from losing her, though he led a quiet, comfortable life here after she died. He always seemed to enjoy our visits. He and our mother—his only niece—were close, and he was very fond of us. He and Aunt Helen never had children of their own, so he sort of claimed our mom as his honorary daughter and us as surrogate grandchildren."

"Does your mother still spend time with you here?"

"We lost our mother three years ago, a little less than a year before Uncle Leo died. She was only fifty-eight. It was very unexpected." She had tried to speak matter-of-factly, but she suspected he heard the faint catch of grief in her voice. She was still feeling a bit misty about that mental image of her mother on the porch.

The quick look of distress in his blue eyes let her know that he had, indeed, heard her pain. He reached out automatically to lay a hand on her shoulder, his palm warm and comforting through the thin fabric of her spring clothing. "I'm sorry, Kinley. I didn't realize—"

With a hard swallow, she shook her head. "Thank-you. I guess I thought you already knew, for some reason."

"No."

She bent a bit too nonchalantly to gently brush a grasshopper off one leg of her slacks, which served the purpose of dislodging Dan's hand from her shoulder. She found it difficult to think clearly and professionally with him touching her that way. Not that she minded, exactly, but better to choose prudence than to let an unguarded moment get away from her.

He shifted obligingly away from her, putting a more comfortable distance between. "Is your father still living?"

Nodding, she straightened, tucking her hands into the pockets of her sweater. "Dad's somewhat of a restless spirit. He and Mom divorced when I was seven and he's traveled a lot since, all around the globe. We see him once a year or so and he calls a couple times a month. He has zero interest in being tied down to any one place, such as running an inn."

She and her siblings had long since acknowledged that their father was never going to change, and had learned to accept their relationship with him for what it was. Cordial, but distant. Disappointing, of course. She was certain that Logan had resented not having his father in his life, though he kept those feelings to himself for the most part, and she thought Bonnie had bonded so closely with Uncle Leo partially to fill that void. As for herself, she'd wondered occasionally if her unsatisfactory connection with her dad had anything to do with her poor choices regarding her unsuccessful marriage, but she didn't let herself dwell on that too often. Now was certainly not the time to do so, she reminded herself, focusing instead on the conversation with Dan.

"None of his kids inherited his wanderlust?"

"I suppose not, though I enjoy taking vacations occasionally. Moving from Tennessee to Virginia to take over the inn was a big adventure for us," she added with a wry laugh.

He fidgeted with his camera. "I guess I have something in common with your dad. I tend to get restless in one place, myself."

She told herself she wasn't disappointed to hear that. Why would she be? Keeping her expression politely interested, she said, "I suppose that's why you chose to be a travel writer."

He grinned. "Well, that—and the fact that my cousin is the managing editor for the magazine. Like you, I can credit family connections for my current career."

Her eyes narrowed. He'd spoken teasingly, but she

couldn't entirely help getting a bit defensive. "We may have gotten our jobs because of family connections, but we are successful at them because of hard work and training," she said, not quite achieving the light tone she attempted.

He seemed to realize his lame joke had fallen flat. "It's obvious that you work extremely hard here. I didn't mean to imply otherwise."

She nodded somewhat stiffly.

Dan made a slow circle to study the grounds. "You've done a great job renovating the place. I can picture it looking very much like this back in the mid-1900s."

He was trying so earnestly to make up for his gaffe that she couldn't help softening a little. "That's the goal. It's an ongoing project, of course, but we're pleased with the progress we've made so far. Let me show you our wedding facilities now."

Shifting his camera to his other hand, he nodded with what might have been relief. "I'd like that."

She backtracked to the deck, explaining that the wedding parties exited the inn through the back door, then descended the right-side stairs which led directly onto the wide, pebbled path to the Queen Anne gazebo. On wedding days, white folding chairs were arranged on either side of the path, forming a central aisle to the gazebo where the officiate would be waiting. Though subject to individual brides' tastes, the decorations generally included garland, candles, flowers, tulle or fairy lights, she added. She didn't mention that the Sossaman wedding would probably feature all the above and then some.

Dan nodded. "Nice setup."

"We've had some beautiful weddings here since we

reopened. And quite a few more booked in coming months." She tried to keep her tone more informative than boastful, but suspected a little of the latter might have crept in. She couldn't help being proud of how much she and her siblings had accomplished in the past two and a half years. "We have several wedding packages available, from full-service with wedding planner, florist, caterer, music and officiate included or customized to the client's specifications. The side lawn will accommodate a large tent that will seat up to 150 guests for a wedding meal. We can even provide chandeliers and an orchestra dais for the tent."

Dan glanced in the direction she'd indicated toward the corner of manicured side lawn visible from where they stood, accessible by three stone steps and a wheelchair ramp. "Did your uncle leave the place in this condition? Eighteen years after closing?"

She grimaced instinctively, but quickly smoothed her expression into a bland smile. "He kept up the basic maintenance, but the decor and gardens had always been Aunt Helen's department."

"So, the answer is no. You and your brother and sister have put a lot of work into the inn and the grounds."

"Yes, we have." Her hands still bore a few small scars from some of the manual labor that had gone into those renovations. She, Bonnie and Logan had all put hours of sweat and effort into the restoration, saving money whenever possible by doing what they could themselves. She figured she would be manning a shovel for the planned koi pond eventually. Considering how much they'd had to do, they still considered it close to a miracle that they'd been able to open only a year after inheriting the place.

"A big investment, too. Must have been intimidating."

"A bit," she said, a major understatement. To help them with the transition, Uncle Leo had made them equal beneficiaries of a generous life insurance policy. Every penny of that had gone into the restoration, along with some extra contributions from their private savings. More than intimidating, the commitment had been terrifying, but Bonnie's persistent optimism had persuaded her siblings to stay the course.

Dan made another, slightly tentative attempt to turn the conversation again into a somewhat more personal direction. "What did you all do before becoming innkeepers? Was it always your plan to reopen the inn?"

She knelt to snap a broken branch from a rosebush. Had someone stepped on the branch? Or was this the work of her brother's dog, Ninja, the bane of her existence? She looked around suspiciously for the mutt, but saw no evidence of him. Logan had promised to keep the dog penned up for the weekend, but Ninja was notorious for escaping the most seemingly secure enclosures.

Remembering that Dan had asked her a question, she straightened and pushed her nemesis to the back of her mind. "Bonnie has a degree in hotel management. Since she was just a kid, it's been her dream to reopen the inn. She worked for an established bed-and-breakfast inn in Knoxville from the time she was in high school all the way through college to prepare herself for this. Even though he didn't want to run it alone, Uncle Leo loved telling stories of the inn in its heyday and it's Bonnie's goal to re-create that time. As you commented yourself, we're well on the way to achieving that end."

Dan nodded toward the tidy caretaker's cottage just visible downhill from the gazebo. "And was it also your brother's dream to run the inn?"

"My brother trained in computer software development and ran his own business for several years. He still works as a small business consultant, but he was ready for a new challenge and the inn came along at just the right time. He's taken on the grounds, and served as the contractor for the construction and remodeling we took on. He's designing plans for the Meditation Garden and another couple of projects we'd like to undertake in the future."

Dan lifted an eyebrow. "Software developer, landscape designer, construction contractor and groundskeeper? That's quite a range of talents."

She smiled and shrugged. "Logan is what you might call multifaceted."

"I look forward to talking with him."

"Oh, I don't think he'll want to be interviewed for your article. My brother prefers to remain in the background." Some people accused Logan of being downright antisocial. He had his reasons, but there were plenty of times when she was exasperated with her brother's muleheadedness.

"You told me earlier that you enjoy the business part of running the inn. That's your background? Business?"

She nodded, comfortable again now that the topic had turned to her work. She never should have let it stray into such personal areas in the first place. "I have a degree in business and a real-estate license. I worked full-time in real-estate sales in Knoxville, Tennessee, until we took over the inn, and I still work part-time for a broker in Blacksburg. I work the occasional open house, take a few listings, do some private showings."

"So both you and your brother have other professional responsibilities outside the inn."

"For now," she conceded lightly. "We both enjoy our other interests."

Whether the inn would ever clear enough to fully support all three of them remained to be seen, but she was satisfied for now that most months ended in the black. The time and financial investments they'd made thus far seemed to be paying off for them. Dan would hear nothing from her that wasn't cheerily positive.

"You put in a lot of hours here and you work part-time selling real estate," Dan remarked after they'd walked together to stand beside the large fountain. Recirculating water spilled musically downward from the six-foot-high top into three increasingly larger fluted bowl-shaped tiers and finally into the shallow pool that surrounded the base. "You're pretty much working seven days a week."

"Pretty much," she answered, smiling to show that she wasn't complaining.

"And what do you do for fun?"

"I enjoy my work. That makes it fun."

Dan shook his head with a chuckle. "Not what I meant."

Absently fishing a leaf from one tier of the fountain, Kinley tried to decide what to do with him next. They had completed the basic tour; it was too early for any of the other scheduled events, and she had a few things on her schedule before lunch. Muffled sounds drifting from the front of the inn indicated that her brother and his crew had already started working on repairs to the portico, which would hinder access there for now. It wasn't that she minded spending time with Dan—just the opposite, in fact—but she had other things to do.

As if in echo of her thoughts, her phone alarm beeped discreetly, reminding her of the meeting with the prospective bridal party who had stayed in the inn last night. She silenced it quickly.

"I don't want to keep you from your plans for the day," Dan assured her. "I know you weren't expecting me until tomorrow. I can entertain myself for the next few hours."

"Yoo-hoo, Kinley. There you are." Eva Sossaman's shrill voice sliced through the peaceful quiet of the gardens as she bustled toward them from the inn with daughter and grandson in tow. "Serena and I were just going to take a few more photos, but I wanted to make sure you remembered to order the patio garlands for the prerehearsal cocktail hour."

Kinley wasn't sure she was entirely successful in swallowing her low groan. Had Dan heard? She spoke quickly. "Yes, of course, Eva. Everything's under control for the wedding. Now, if you'll excuse us, Mr. Phelan and I have a meeting scheduled. Please let Bonnie or Rhoda know if there's anything at all you need before you go."

"Oh. Yes, of course." Eva looked disappointed that Kinley was taking the handsome writer away when she would probably have loved to entertain him with endless descriptions of the upcoming wedding.

"I'll see you later," Kinley promised, edging toward the inn and nodding discreetly at Dan to accompany her.

"But I—"

Eva's attempt at protest was interrupted by a splash

from the fountain behind them. They all turned to see Grayson standing in the shallow pool at the base, stomping the water with his now-sodden sneakers, bending to reach for one of the pennies someone had tossed into the pool.

Eva shrieked. "Grayson! Oh, my sweet stars, what on earth were you thinking? Serena, get him out of there."

But Dan had already moved to skillfully pluck the child from the pool. He held the dripping imp at arm's length, his mouth quirked into a crooked grin that Kinley found almost impossible not to reciprocate when their eyes met over the boy's head. With an effort, she kept her expression schooled. Pressing a button on her phone with her thumb, she lifted the phone to her ear, speaking to Eva as she did so. "I'll have Rhoda bring out some towels and help you dry him off."

Mumbling what might have been thanks or apologies or a jumbled mixture of both, Serena took her nephew from Dan and set him firmly on the pebbled path while Eva continued to scold the child, who looked not at all penitent. In fact, he seemed to be interested in climbing back into the fountain, being held back only by his aunt's firm hands.

Kinley knew the boy would soon turn five, but she thought privately that he acted more like a toddler at times. Probably because his grandmother let him get away with so much, despite her show of fussing at him. Kinley didn't have kids of her own, of course, and maybe never would, but she could tell when a child was being overly indulged.

Assured that Rhoda was on her way with the towels, and that Serena had convinced her mother that they should take the boy home immediately, Kinley hurried Dan away before they could be detained again. She was not at all happy with the way the day had progressed thus far. She would feel much better once she had regained control and gotten back onto her carefully planned schedule.

"So, we have a meeting?" Dan asked as soon as they were inside the inn again.

She wrinkled her nose in response to his tongue-in-cheek tone. "It was the first excuse that came to me. I didn't think you'd really want to spend the next hour or more hearing about Serena's wedding plans."

He chuckled, a rich, deep sound that made her tummy do a funny little tap dance. "I'm pretty good at getting myself out of things I don't want to do. I'd have found an excuse for Mrs. Sossaman. But thanks for the rescue, anyway."

She glanced past him when a foursome came noisily down the stairs. She greeted them with a smile. "Here you are. I'm ready for our meeting. Dan Phelan, this is Stephanie Engel, her fiancé, Richard Molaro, and Stephanie's mother and sister, Faye Engel and Jennifer Vines. Stephanie and Richard are considering having their wedding here at Bride Mountain Inn."

"It is a beautiful setting for a wedding," he said with a flash of charming smile, earning himself a few more bonus points in Kinley's esteem.

"We agree," Richard said with a besotted glance toward his fiancée. "We're ready to book the date and discuss options."

Pleased, Kinley motioned toward a doorway behind them. "Let's go into the office and get started, shall we? Dan—"

"I'll catch up with you later," he said, taking a step

backward. "I have some notes to write. I'll leave you to plan what will surely be a beautiful wedding for a beautiful bride."

His easy tone and charming wink made the young bride-to-be giggle rather than groan at the blatant flattery. Her cheeks were glowing when she hurried through the office door Kinley had just opened for them. Kinley waited to follow them in, speaking to Dan. "Do you have plans for lunch?"

"No, I don't."

"If you like, we can meet here in the foyer at noon and I'll take you to Bride Mountain Café for a meal and to answer more of your questions. My treat." That would allow her an hour for the meeting, which she was sure would be sufficient. She considered her friend Liza Miller's café another enticing reason to stay at the inn. Less than half a mile away, it was close enough to walk, if the guests desired, and provided food that always left them raving. Having Dan mention the café favorably in his article could only benefit both businesses.

He nodded agreeably. "See you at noon."

With that, he turned and ran lightly up the stairs toward his room. Suddenly realizing that she was watching his tight backside, she blinked rapidly and turned toward the office. Time to get back to work, which meant putting all thoughts of sexy travel writers out of her mind for the next hour or so—though she couldn't help looking forward to that lunch with an anticipation that didn't feel at all professional.

The Engel-Molaro party checked out of the inn immediately following the very productive meeting. Kinley and Bonnie ushered them out the side door, repeating assurances that they would not regret booking their wedding here at Bride Mountain Inn. The sisters shared big, satisfied smiles when the door had closed behind their departing guests.

"That's going to be a great gig," Kinley predicted smugly. "Stephanie seems unlikely to turn into a bridezilla, Richard had some excellent suggestions and Stephanie's mom and sister appear content to leave the arrangements to the bridal couple. Not to mention that they're considering purchasing the full wedding package from us."

They exchanged a quick, jubilant high five. A few more bookings like that, Kinley thought, and they could order the supplies for the Meditation Garden. Another good year after this one and they'd start thinking seriously about expansion plans—a couple of honeymoon cottages, perhaps. Knowing how driven she could be, her sister and brother expressed apprehension every time she started talking about those possible future developments, but that didn't stop her from dreaming big.

"Am I interrupting a celebration?" Dan asked from the stairs.

Bonnie giggled, but Kinley transitioned smoothly into business mode. "Dan and I are going to the café for lunch. Do you want to join us, Bonnie?"

"Thanks, but I have things to do here. If you need anything or have any questions for me later, Dan, I'll be around."

"Thank you. My room is very comfortable, by the way. You've done a great job decorating."

Bonnie's face turned pink with pleasure. The way to her sister's heart was definitely through compliments to the inn, Kinley thought with a slight frown. It didn't hurt, of course, that the nice words came from a totally sexy guy.

She cleared her throat and motioned toward the side door. "We'll have to go out this way. Bonnie, I have my phone if you need me."

"I'll take care of things here. You just go enjoy your lunch with Dan."

Something in Bonnie's tone made Kinley eye her suspiciously, but her sister merely gave her a blandly innocent smile in return. With a slight shake of her head, Kinley led their guest outside, determined to remain in control of this somewhat hectic day.

The chill of the spring morning had been replaced by a pleasant warmth fanned by a slight breeze that tossed Kinley's hair around her face the moment she stepped out onto the side porch. She reached up to tuck a strand behind her ear, then pushed the sleeves of her light cardigan above her elbows. As always, she wore stylish but comfortable shoes, so the half-mile distance to the café wasn't a concern when she asked, "Shall we walk or drive? Or we keep a half dozen loaner bicycles available for guests if you prefer to bike."

"Whichever you prefer," Dan replied gallantly.

"Let's walk, then. It's such a pretty day." And she could use the exercise to clear her mind, she thought. For some reason, she had a little trouble thinking clearly when he looked at her with those strikingly blue eyes.

Chapter Three

As he and Kinley walked past the front of the inn on the way to lunch, Dan saw that some progress had been made in the repairs to the portico even during the relatively short time since he had arrived. The truck had been moved and the sagging portico had been jacked up to level again. A weathered-looking man who appeared to be in his late forties or early fifties, wearing faded, hard-used jeans and a stained gray T-shirt that displayed strong arms and a beer belly, balanced on a ladder, carefully reattaching dislodged gingerbread trim. A younger, thinner man in a Virginia Tech T-shirt and baggy shorts waited at the base of the ladder with a toolbox. Logan Carmichael stood nearby, talking on his phone.

Logan completed the call as Kinley and Dan passed, shoving his phone into a belt holster and speaking gruffly to his sister. "The new post is on the way. Hank had a spare available, as I thought. Everything will be back in place in time for the wedding rehearsal tomorrow evening."

"That's great news," his sister said with relief. She motioned toward Dan. "We're going for lunch. Want to join us?"

Dan wasn't surprised when Logan shook his head. "I'm going to finish up here with Curtis and Zach."

Kinley nodded as though she, too, had expected that reply. "Okay, see you later."

Logan had already turned away to get back to work. Shaking her head slightly in an apparent response to her brother's brusqueness, Kinley fell into step beside Dan on the driveway toward the road. There was no sidewalk to the café, but the paved road was wide enough for pedestrian safety and dead-ended at the inn, so there was little traffic. Spring-flowering trees and native bushes grew on the hillsides along the roadway, and the sky above had deepened to a rich, cloudless blue. Dan couldn't have special-ordered a nicer day for a leisurely walk with the oh-so-interesting Kinley Carmichael.

He'd noticed the Bride Mountain Café on his drive up to the inn earlier. The diner was on the smaller side, nondescript in architectural style, but sparkling windows and fluttering green canopies gave it a welcoming appearance. It looked clean and inviting, with enough cars in the tidy lot to demonstrate its popularity with the locals. It also couldn't hurt that the next closest eating establishment was probably a good three miles away, he thought.

The café was busy, but not overly crowded on this Thursday lunch hour, so he and Kinley were seated immediately. She seemed to know everyone who worked there and several of the other diners, as she was greeted by name with smiles and waves. A thirtysomething woman with intricately styled hair and warm, dark chocolate eyes, wearing a plastic tag engraved with the name Mary, handed them each a menu.

Kinley introduced him to the server, then asked, "Is Liza here? I want Dan to meet her."

"No, she had to leave for a little while. She had an appointment in town," Mary replied. "I'll give y'all a couple of minutes to look at the menu and then I'll be back for your orders. Not that you need to look at the menu," she added with a wink for Kinley. "I imagine you have it memorized."

"Pretty much," Kinley agreed with a laugh. She looked across the table at Dan when the server moved to another group of customers. "Liza Miller owns the café. She's a good friend. I hope you have a chance to meet her while you're staying at the inn."

"I'm sure I'll be back here in the next day or two. I'll introduce myself to her if you aren't with me, and I'll definitely mention the diner when I write the article."

His words obviously pleased her. She explained that Bride Mountain Café was best known for its soup-and-sandwich combos, and everything was made in-house, even the bread. The café was open for lunch and early dinner, from eleven until eight Monday through Saturday. "Though we serve only breakfast at the inn most days, we provide a big brunch and a light supper on Sundays," she added. "Between our schedule and the café hours, our guests can enjoy every meal without getting into a car, if they like."

His mouth quirked into a half smile in response to

her practiced spiel. "You've thought of every detail, haven't you?"

She seemed oblivious to his irony. "We certainly try."

Glancing at the menu again, he asked, "What do you recommend?"

"I really like the chicken tortilla soup with a quesadilla, which is today's special. My brother is partial to the loaded-baked-potato soup with a Virginia ham sandwich. Bonnie loves the minestrone with the eggplant-and-artichoke panini. Honestly, you can't really go wrong. It's all good."

Dan had listened attentively to her recitation. When she finished, he said, "You actually have memorized the menu, haven't you? You sounded like a radio ad."

She frowned just a bit, as if trying to decide if he was making fun of her. He wasn't mocking her, of course, but he couldn't help teasing her a little, just to try to coax her out of that strictly business mode she seemed to fall into so naturally.

Quickly smoothing her expression, she gave him a bland smile. "All entirely sincere, I assure you. I wouldn't eat here so often if I didn't genuinely enjoy the food."

"And you wouldn't have brought me here if you didn't think I'd like it, too." He had no doubt that her invitation to lunch had been as much a marketing move as a gracious one.

"Um, right."

Only when they'd ordered and their food had been served did Kinley get around to asking something she'd probably been wondering all morning. "So how did you end up arriving here a day early?"

He chuckled. "Long story. Short version is, I drove

up from Atlanta to Charlotte yesterday expecting to spend at least part of today interviewing a museum curator in Charlotte. That interview fell through at the last minute. I woke up in a particularly uncomfortable motel bed at five this morning and decided on impulse to make the drive to the inn. As I said earlier, I figured I'd either spend an extra night at the inn or find a room nearby until my scheduled arrival time. I'm glad you had a room for me. The bed looks a heck of a lot more comfortable than the one I tried to sleep in last night."

"I hope it will be." As if she were suddenly a bit too warm, she pushed up her sleeves. "If there's anything at all you need to make your stay more pleasant, please let us know."

"You're certainly making it very pleasant so far," he said, unable to resist adding a smile just a touch too personal to be considered strictly business. Maybe she already sensed he was attracted to her. Was it strictly wishful thinking on his part that she was aware of him in that way, too?

His instincts were usually pretty good in that regard, but Kinley was a bit hard to read. She was so intensely, almost amusingly, focused on presenting a positive spin for his article. And even though he told himself to follow her lead and keep his own feelings reined in, there was just something about her that tempted him to forget he was with her only on assignment for his job.

"Congratulations on your new wedding booking, by the way." He could still easily picture the jubilant, unself-conscious smile she'd exchanged with her sister when she'd closed the door behind the future wedding party, before she had realized he was there to see her. He'd like to see that carefree side of her again.

"Thank you." Setting down her tea glass, she picked up her soup spoon. "Are there any other questions I can answer for you now?"

"A few." There was quite a lot he'd like to know about her, but he'd content himself with a few random queries now.

She nodded encouragingly. "Feel free."

He asked the first thing that popped into his head. "What's your favorite color?"

The faintest of frowns appeared between her tidily arched brows. "Moss green. The color we chose for the upstairs hallway of the inn, actually. Bonnie let me pick that one."

"Favorite candy?"

"My sister's homemade peanut brittle. She makes it sometimes for our guests to enjoy in the evenings around the game tables. We—"

"Favorite musical group?"

"I, uh—Black Lab." She couldn't seem to think of a way to turn that answer into a plug for the inn. "What do these questions have to do with—"

"Which do you like better, football or soccer?"

She laughed softly then, as if she couldn't quite help doing so, and the musical sound was a nice reward for his persistence. "I grew up in Tennessee. So, football. Is there a point to this interrogation?"

He flashed a grin at her. "Just checking to see if you're always in business mode. So you do have outside interests?"

"Of course." She touched the corners of her mouth with her napkin. "But you aren't here to write about me. My sister, brother and I are equal partners in the inn."

"One more personal question?"

She eyed him warily. "That depends on what it is."

"Is there a Mr. Kinley?" The answer to this question, of course, was more relevant than his professional ethics to whether he would continue flirting with her. He might be somewhat lax in his work habits, especially compared with what he'd seen of Kinley thus far, but he wasn't a jerk.

"Not anymore, there isn't." She changed the subject with a firmness that told him there was a lot more to that story. "What else would you like to know about the inn?"

Sensing the invisible barrier she'd just erected between them on that personal topic, he obligingly backed off. "Tell me more about the inn's history. You said your mother's uncle inherited it from his father, the original owner."

Looking relieved to be back on topic, Kinley nodded and spoke more comfortably. "Yes. My great-grandfather Finley had two sons, Leo and my mother's father, Stuart. Stuart died when my mother was just a toddler. Her mother wasn't interested in staying in Virginia, so she moved back to Tennessee to be closer to her own family. My grandmother remarried and settled down in the Knoxville area. She had two more children with no biological connection to the inn. Every summer during her childhood and teen years, my mother came back here to Virginia to stay with her paternal grandparents and with Uncle Leo and Aunt Helen, who were all running the inn together during that time. When Mom's grandfather died, he left the inn to Uncle Leo, who had been running it almost exclusively for several years by that time."

"And your great-uncle, who had no children of his

own, kept it in the family by leaving it to his niece's kids when he passed."

She nodded in approval that he'd followed along. "Yes."

"It's great that you have that connection to your family's past. I'm sure your mother would have been very proud of what you and your sister and brother have accomplished in the past two and a half years."

He'd spoken somewhat artlessly and almost immediately second-guessed his words, hoping she didn't take them as patronizing. But she seemed pleased, instead, by the sentiment, seeming to sense his sincerity.

"I think she would be proud," she said quietly. "Uncle Leo, too.

Dan reached for his tea glass. "Must be a nice feeling. Knowing your parents are proud of you, I mean."

She cocked her head, and he wondered if she'd heard more in his offhanded comment than he'd intended to reveal. "Are your parents still living?"

"Yes." He saw no need to elaborate just then about his father's rapidly failing health, nor to go into details about his strained relationship with them.

"I'm sure they're proud of you, too. After you contacted me, I read quite a few of your articles. You have a very nice way with words. It's obvious that you work hard to bring the venues you've visited to life for your readers."

Her compliment pleased him more than it probably should have. His overachieving, overdemanding parents would beg to disagree with her reference to his hard work, but he was glad to hear her acknowledge that writing travel articles wasn't quite the fluff job his folks considered it to be. He did work hard at crafting his articles, whether they focused on pretty wedding venues or Southern adventure vacations like white-water rafting or mountain biking. Maybe he preferred to be on a bike or in a kayak rather than talking about rose gardens and Queen Anne gazebos, but he put equal amounts of effort into the stories. He labored as diligently with those articles as he did with the novel he'd wanted to write for a long time, having just been waiting for what seemed like the right time to dedicate himself to completing the project.

Because he wasn't particularly comfortable discussing his complicated standing with his parents, he was rather relieved when Mary appeared at their table just then to collect their plates. "Did you save room for dessert? We make the best pies in the whole state."

"They do," Kinley seconded. "I'm partial to fruit pies, myself, but their cream pies are especially popular with the majority of their customers."

Dan declined politely. "I'll try the pie another time. I'm a little full right now."

"You should come back," Mary encouraged with a big smile. "It'd be a shame if your article didn't mention our famous pies."

"Then I'll be sure and try a slice or two before I leave the area," he promised.

Kinley laid her napkin on the table. "I'll take the check, Mary."

Mary placed the vinyl folder into Kinley's open hand. "Did you tell your writer friend about the ghost?"

Ghost? Intrigued, Dan lifted an eyebrow.

Kinley made a little sound that might have been a swallowed protest. That tiny frown was back between her eyebrows. "We haven't talked about any old legends of the area," she said lightly. "That's not really the type of story Dan is here to write."

Taking Kinley's payment, Mary winked at Dan. "Ask her to tell you about the bride. There's still a few folks around here that are fascinated by the old tale. Some even claim to have seen her. If you can't get the story out of Kinley, come back tomorrow and I'll tell you while you sample our pies."

"I'll tell him about it." Kinley pushed back her chair. "It's just a fanciful old story, Dan. I doubt you'll find it particularly interesting."

"I'd like to hear it." He rose as she did, speaking to Mary on the way out. "The food was delicious. I'll definitely be back."

"I'm sure Liza would love to meet you. Bye, now. Y'all have a nice afternoon."

He recognized the middle-aged couple who entered the café as he and Kinley were leaving. They were guests at the inn. Honeymooners, he'd been told. He nodded to them as Kinley greeted them in passing, pausing long enough to recommend the tortilla soup and quesadilla combo. The café owner really should reimburse Kinley for her endorsements, he thought with a private smile. She was almost as enthusiastic about the café menu as she was the inn's offerings. He hoped her friend Liza reciprocated the business plugs.

"So about this ghost bride…" he said when they were headed back toward the inn.

Kinley wrinkled her nose. "Like I said, it's just an old legend. I'm not even sure when it started. Decades ago. Probably someone's whimsical way of explaining the name of the mountain, since no one seems to know exactly when or why it got the name Bride Mountain.

I've always suspected it evolved from the name of an early landowner. There are several McBride families found around this part of the country. Or maybe someone built an early house here for his bride and called it that. Or maybe someone thought the morning fog looked like a bridal veil around the top of the mountain. Who knows?"

"The ghost?" he prodded gently, risking another frown.

He got a faint sigh, instead. "Some people claim to have seen the spirit of a woman in bridal white on the mountain, usually on the grounds of the inn. Legend has it that couples who see her are destined to be together in a happily-ever-after union. Part ghost story, part fairy tale, right?"

"Have many people claimed to see the woman in white?"

She appeared to concentrate very hard on where she placed her steps as they trudged up the hill. "Not many. A few over the years."

"Anyone you know?"

He heard her clear her throat before she answered. "Uncle Leo swore that he and Aunt Helen saw the bride the night he proposed to her in the rose garden behind the inn."

He found that fascinating. "No kidding."

"I've always been pretty sure Uncle Leo made up the story to entertain us as children," she said quickly, looking surprisingly unenchanted by the tale. "Bonnie, especially, loved to hear him tell it and asked him to do so every time we saw him. He embellished the story a little more every time he told it. If he did see something that night, it was probably just a trick of the mist, misinterpreted by a blissful young couple who'd grown up hearing about the bride and had just gotten engaged."

He stopped walking to face her more fully, cocking his head to closely study her face. "Why does it bother you so much to talk about this? I could tell you didn't like Mary mentioning the ghost and you're doing everything you can to discourage my interest in the subject."

She reached up to her breeze-tossed hair, trying to smooth it into her usual sleek, asymmetrical bob. "The main reason, of course, is that I don't believe in ghosts."

"What about fairy tales?"

"I'm not a big fan of those, either," she admitted.

Interesting. Was her disillusionment a result of the former "Mr. Kinley" she'd alluded to? Had some jerk broken spunky Kinley Carmichael's heart? The possibility made him unexpectedly, disproportionately angry. Just what was going on here, anyway? He reminded himself that he barely knew the woman, though his enthrallment with her had been instant and powerful, for some reason. Had he been the fanciful type, he might have wondered if there was some sort of romantic charm attached to Bride Mountain Inn.

Trying to keep his attention on the topic at hand, he said, "Still, maybe a mention of the ghost bride would be a boost to your business. A pretty wedding venue with a romantic legend attached? Sounds like quite a draw."

She shook her head firmly. "Back in the early 1960s, a woman who claimed to be a psychic visited the inn and said she had seen and talked with the ghost. She put out a cockamamy story about a woman who died the night before her wedding to her one true love. Now, supposedly, the bride appears to bless those couples she deems are meant to be together as she and her love couldn't be on this earthly plane. The story appeared in an obscure magazine and wasn't widely publicized, but even that amount of attention caused problems for the inn."

"How so?"

She shrugged. "It was the sixties. Uncle Leo said a bunch of 'hippie new agers' camped out on the grounds, hoping to see the ghost and generally causing trouble. Once he took care of that problem, they had the occasional attention-seeking couple who either insisted they'd seen the bride and wanted publicity about it, or brides who became very upset because they *didn't* see her and decided that was a bad omen for their weddings. That's why I try to downplay the legend whenever anyone asks me about it. I can't stop you from mentioning it in your article, of course, but I wish you wouldn't make it the main theme of your story."

He didn't appreciate being told how to do his job, any more than Kinley would like it if he did the same to her. He admired her dedication to her work, but there was such a thing as carrying business too far—a concept his workaholic parents had never quite understood.

"I have done a series on supposedly haunted places in the South, and I'll probably do other articles in that vein," he answered evenly, his tone a bit clipped. "This isn't that kind of assignment. The series that will include your inn is focused on nice places to hold weddings. We've already vetted the settings, so the reviews will all be positive, which is the tone my editor wants to set. If a mention of the old legend, even a tongue-in-cheek reference, makes my article more interesting, I'll use it, but it will not detract from the tangible, factual reasons future brides should choose your inn as a setting for their weddings."

He could tell she wasn't entirely satisfied, but she kept her tone determinedly cordial. "I'd much rather the inn be known for the excellent amenities we work so hard to provide than for some creepy old ghost story."

He shook his head, pushing aside the irritation and offering a wry smile. "Has anyone ever accused you of having a few control issues?"

She looked taken aback for a moment, then gave him an answering smile that was decidedly rueful. "Occasionally. I prefer to think of it as knowing exactly what I want and making sure I get it."

On an impulse, he reached out to catch a strand of hair that was blowing around her face and tuck it tidily behind her left ear. "I guess I can understand that. I go after what I want, too."

She studied his face, obviously trying to decide exactly how to respond. He found it encouraging that she didn't immediately step away from him. Not for the first time, he sensed that his attraction was reciprocated, at least to an extent—even if perhaps hesitantly on Kinley's part.

With some regret, he watched her settle her expression into her usual friendly mask, carefully hiding any thoughts that had nothing to do with business. "We should get back to the inn. I have a few more things to do this afternoon."

He nodded and turned to face uphill again. He froze before taking a step, his gaze locked on the unsettling image ahead. It wasn't a ghost he saw facing them on the side of the road. This creature, he thought with a swallow, looked more like a hound from hell. And it was moving toward them with narrowed eyes and a low, raspy sound emerging from its massive throat.

Every nerve ending on alert, he moved to position himself between the animal and Kinley. Not that he had the first clue what he would do if it attacked.

Swallowing a groan, Kinley reached out to nudge Dan gently from in front of her. She felt the rigidity of his muscles beneath his turned-up shirtsleeve and knew he was braced to protect her. As much as she prided herself on her competence and independence, she still felt a tiny thrill of feminine pleasure in response to his gallantry, though it was entirely unnecessary this time.

"It's okay, Dan," she said. "Unfortunately, I know this ugly mutt."

Making the rumbly growly sound that was his weird way of greeting people he knew, the black-and-brown dog paused in front of her and dropped something at her feet. She sighed heavily when she saw that it was one of her sister's nicest gardening gloves. "Bonnie is not going to be happy to have your slobber all over her glove," she muttered, bending to gingerly retrieve the soggy mitt.

"This is your dog?" Dan sounded a little sheepish about his reaction to his first sight of the shaggy animal.

She straightened, then shook her head in exasperation when the dog leaned his solid body companionably against her thigh, making her stumble a bit to keep her balance. "Logan calls him Ninja, because of his mostly black color and the marking that looks like a mask across his eyes. And also because it's almost impossible to keep him restrained."

"So he's your brother's dog."

"He showed up at the inn during the winter, cold and hungry and obviously a stray. Logan fed him a few times and he stayed. There's a chain link fence around the backyard of the caretaker's cottage, mostly to keep out wild animals from the woods, and Logan put a nice doghouse back there for Ninja. But he should have named him Houdini, because the dumb dog keeps getting out and causing problems at the inn—stealing stuff like this glove, picking flowers, playing in the fountain and intimidating guests who catch a glimpse of his ugly mug, even though we've never seen him show any signs of aggression."

"Guess he's not so dumb, after all." Visibly relaxed now, Dan extended a friendly hand to the dog, who sniffed it, licked it, then butted his broad head against it in a blatant hint for an ear rub. "Um, why is he growling at me?"

Kinley laughed wryly. "He never barks, but he makes that rumbly sound when he's happy. Bonnie says he's purring, like a cat. Crazy mutt."

Bending to rub the wagging dog's ears with both hands, Dan grinned. "So, what breed do you think he is?"

"Logan guesses part Rottweiler, part Lab and a few mystery genes that I think include imp and demon."

Laughing, Dan gave the dog one last rub and straightened, absently brushing his hands on his pants. "He seems like a nice enough fellow to me."

"That might be true if he would stay where he's supposed to be. Popping up unexpectedly to unnerve the guests is hardly good for business, even though we try to remember to inform everyone checking in that my brother has a dog who poses no threat to them. To be honest, I've attempted to talk Logan into finding another home for Ninja. Logan says he tried at the beginning, but no one else wanted him, and now I think they've bonded. I am going to insist now that he should reinforce the fence, both for the safety of the dog and for the comfort of our guests."

"Sounds reasonable."

They resumed their walk back to the inn with Ninja plodding companionably beside them. Kinley hoped the wandering dog would join the list of things Dan would not feel compelled to mention in his article.

Very little about her interactions with him thus far had gone exactly as she'd planned. He wasn't at all what she had expected, and she certainly couldn't have predicted—or controlled—the other minor glitches since he'd arrived. She could only hope the next few days while he was here would go as smoothly as possible. And that she would manage to resist his seemingly habitual flirtation. She knew better than to take him seriously. Even if he found her attractive, which seemed to be true, it didn't mean he had any intention of doing anything about it. A few laughs, a few exchanged smiles—at the most a few days of a lighthearted fling—and then he would move on to the next assignment, the next willing woman. At least, that was what she surmised about him, based on painful past experience.

That wasn't the way she rolled, she assured herself. She would stay firmly in command of herself while he was here.

The new post lay on the drive next to the jack and two-by-four rig that currently supported the portico. Logan, Curtis and Zach sat in rockers on the porch eating sandwiches and drinking iced tea that Bonnie had

most likely provided for them. Seeing the trio approaching him, Logan grimaced, set his empty tea glass aside
and stood. "Where did you find him?"

"He found us," Kinley replied. "Halfway down the
road to the café. I take it you didn't know he was out?"

"Obviously. I wouldn't let him wander down the
road," Logan muttered with a scowl. He reached down
to loop two fingers beneath the dog's leather collar. "I'll
take him back to my yard. Curtis, Zach, y'all finish up
your lunches and then we'll get that post in place. We'll
get it caulked and primed this afternoon and paint it in
the morning."

Kinley liked the sound of that. Barring any unfore-
seen complications, the front of the inn should be fully
restored by the time the Sossaman-Thompson wedding
party arrived for rehearsal, which should mollify Eva.
She would probably find something else to criticize or
complain about, but that was one issue out of the way.

"I hope you can figure out how he escaped this time,"
she said to her brother. "We really can't risk having
him disrupt a wedding rehearsal or even scare guests
who are just trying to take a walk through the garden."

He'd heard that speech probably a dozen times since
he'd taken in the stray dog, but she felt compelled to
remind him again what was at stake. She didn't even
want to think how Eva would react if this hulk of a dog
interrupted the rehearsal—or even worse, she thought
with a slight shudder, the wedding.

Logan gave her a look over his shoulder and started
to speak, then stopped himself with a visible effort,
probably because he remembered that Dan was within
hearing. She would probably get a lecture later about
her habitually bossy tendencies. Maybe after he'd gotten

that off his chest, she would suggest again that he should try to find a more suitable home for the dog. Surely someone wanted a Rottweiler-Lab-imp-demon mix.

Dan glanced at Kinley when Logan led the dog out of sight. "Your brother is limping. Do you think he hurt himself this morning?"

"No, he's had the limp for several years." She motioned toward the porch without elaborating. "Shall we go in?"

"I'm sure you have things to do this afternoon," Dan said when they entered the dining room through the side door. "Don't let me keep you from them."

"I should get back to my to-do list," she agreed. "What will you do?"

"I think I'll drive around the area. Check out some of the local flavor. Maybe visit one or two of those museums, myself."

"We'd love to have you for dinner this evening, Dan," Bonnie said from the doorway into the foyer. "Logan, Kinley and I will be dining in my apartment downstairs at six. Nothing fancy, but there will be plenty of food, if you'd like to join us."

"That's sounds great, if you don't think your brother will mind."

"Of course Logan won't mind," Bonnie assured him with a smile.

Dan grinned back at her. "Then I'll be there. Thank you, Miss Bonnie."

Bonnie giggled. Kinley tried not to scowl. "If you two will excuse me, I have some calls to make."

It was a very good thing, she told herself as she headed rapidly toward the office, that she hadn't taken Dan's flirting seriously. If she had, she just might be feeling a bit envious of the smile he'd just given her sister. Which, of course, she wasn't. Not at all, she assured herself.

She closed the office door behind her with a bit more of a sharp snap than she had intended.

Chapter Four

That evening, Dan tapped on the door of Bonnie's basement apartment. She welcomed him in with a warm smile, informing him that her siblings were on their way. Her living quarters included an airy, open kitchen-dining-living area, and she told him there were two bedrooms with en suite baths. Her decorating skills were obvious here, too, with pale colors and light woods making the limited space feel bigger and very comfortable. Windows brought in light on two sides of the apartment and lamps had been used judiciously to brighten dark corners.

Logan arrived only minutes after Bonnie ushered Dan in and served him a glass of freshly made lemonade. He didn't look surprised to see Dan there, so he must have been warned ahead. But then again, Logan Carmichael hid his thoughts so well that Dan wasn't sure he'd have known if the guy was surprised or not. Logan, too, accepted a glass of lemonade.

Bonnie waved them toward the seating area. "You guys make yourselves comfortable. Kinley's running a little late and I have just a couple things to finish up in the kitchen before we eat."

Dan noticed Logan's slight limp again when they moved to sit. The hitch was in his left leg, as if the knee didn't quite fully extend. An old sports injury, perhaps? He could see this rock-solid-looking guy as an athlete. Logan sat on the couch and Dan sank into a nearby chair.

"I saw the front of the inn a little while ago when I got back from a sightseeing drive," he said to initiate a conversation. "You got a lot done today. The new post looks good."

Logan nodded. "Fortunately, there wasn't much damage. It was easy enough to jack up the corner and slide a new post into place. Reconnecting the gingerbread without breaking it further was the biggest challenge."

"Kinley told me you're a software designer in addition to your duties here. What sort of programs do you write?"

Lowering his lemonade glass after taking a long sip, Logan shrugged. "I'm more of a consultant these days. I customize software for specific customer needs. Small businesses, mostly."

"Interesting."

"Better than working in a cubicle," the other man replied laconically.

Dan lifted his glass in an implied toast. "I hear you on that."

With a rusty-sounding chuckle, Logan raised his own glass, then took a drink.

Kinley rushed in the door then, her phone to her ear. She waved a greeting to Dan and Logan while tossing her purse on the floor beside the couch. She moved to the far side of the room to continue her conversation. Giving her privacy, Dan continued his talk with her brother. "Did you figure out how your dog got out of your yard?"

"I think someone must have let him out," Logan answered with a frustrated shake of his head. "I walked that damned fence line twice and there were no breaks. Someone had to open the gate."

"You think it might have been one of the guests?"

"Oh, I can't imagine one of the guests would have done that," Kinley said, sliding her phone into her pocket and speaking before her brother could answer. "But I hope you put a lock on the gate, just in case, Logan."

"The tool shed is in my backyard. Zach and Curtis and I don't want to stop to punch in a combination or dig out a key every time we need a hammer or a pair of garden shears," he grumbled. "I tightened the latch and hung a private-property, keep-out sign on the fence. I printed a note on the sign saying to keep the gate closed because of the dog. I'll keep an eye on my place, but that should take care of any overly curious guests."

Kinley didn't look entirely satisfied, but she nodded and put on a smile for Dan's benefit. "I'm sorry I was late. I've got a couple making an offer on a house this evening and the owners are putting together a counter-offer. I'll probably have another call or two this evening, so I'll apologize in advance."

"What else is new?" Logan asked drily.

Pointedly ignoring her brother, she turned toward the kitchen. "What can I do to help, Bonnie?"

"You can chop the tomatoes for the salad," Bonnie said from in front of the far counter, where she was ladling something from a large, stainless steel slow cooker onto a big platter.

"Dan, how was your afternoon?" Kinley asked, raising her voice enough to be heard over the brisk sound of chopping. "Did you make it to one of the museums?"

"Yes, I did. I spent a little time at the Great Lakes to Florida Highway Museum, the one set up in the old gas station. It was an interesting look back at 1920s and 30s transportation. I had a college friend whose dad collected old oil cans and petroleum advertising products. He'd love the displays I saw this afternoon."

"Are you interested in history, Dan?" Bonnie asked, looking up from her preparations.

"Yes. I took a lot of history classes in college. They've come in handy in some of my articles."

"Have you ever considered writing fiction?"

He hesitated a moment before answering. Usually he brushed off similar questions and quickly changed the subject. The story that had been germinating in his imagination, growing increasingly demanding of his attention during the past months, was something he'd kept to himself, with only very few exceptions. He wasn't sure why he was so reluctant to admit he had started a novel. Because it seemed like such a private goal, perhaps? Out of concern that he would never actually finish the book, leaving others skeptical about his level of commitment? Or—he shifted uncomfortably in his seat—was a fear of failure, of the type of doubt and disapproval he'd sensed so often from his parents, always at the back of his mind when it came to his own dreams?

"As a matter of fact, yes," he said, almost surprising himself. He wasn't sure whether it was because Bonnie had a way of drawing others into conversation, or because Kinley was so obviously paying close attention, but he felt the need to answer candidly with them, rather than prevaricating. "I have a book idea I've been playing with for the past few months."

He saw Kinley shoot a look at him from the chopping board, her eyebrows lifted with interest. She wasn't contributing much to the conversation, but he knew she wasn't missing a word of it as she chopped tomatoes and piled them into the salad.

"Oh, that's exciting." Delicious aromas wafted from the large platter Bonnie carried to the already set table. "Where did you go to college?"

."Bama," he said, using the popular nickname for the University of Alabama. "Roll, Tide."

Logan made a sound similar to his dog's rumble-growl.

Dan chuckled and glanced at the other man, remembering where Kinley had said she and her siblings had grown up. "Let me guess, University of Tennessee?"

"Go, Vols," Logan said in confirmation.

"No sports rivalry at my dinner table," Bonnie ordered, lighting two white tapers in milk-glass holders. Though she'd tried to sound stern, her smile gave her away. "Do you still live in Alabama, Dan? The magazine is headquartered in Hoover, right?"

"It is. I keep a small apartment in Hoover, not that I'm there much."

"Is that where you grew up?"

"Yeah, we lived in the suburban Birmingham area." And he had always chafed to get away from there, dreaming of someday living in L.A. or New York or even Europe—anywhere but Alabama. Anywhere but under his parents' thumbs. His plans hadn't worked out that way, but he had compromised by taking the travel job offered by his cousin, an ambitious and determined woman almost twenty years his senior who'd founded her own modestly successful magazine at a time when magazines were generally expected to fail.

"Do you still have family in Birm—"

Bonnie's polite question was cut off by a cry of pain from Kinley.

Reacting swiftly, Dan reached Kinley's side at the same time as her siblings. She had dropped the knife and grabbed a kitchen towel, which she'd wrapped around her left hand. Most of the tomato was already in the salad bowl, but one small section sat partially chopped on the cutting board, surrounded by several bright red drops of blood.

"How bad is it?" Logan demanded, reaching for his sister's hand.

Holding her towel-bundled hand out of his reach, Kinley looked chagrined when she met Dan's eyes. "It's fine. I just need to stick a bandage on it. I didn't get any blood in the salad."

"We can see that," he assured her. "Why don't you let your brother look at your cut?"

Bonnie dashed across the room. "I'll bring the first-aid kit," she called back over her shoulder.

Noticing Kinley looked a little pale, Dan motioned toward the table. "Sit down. I'll get you a glass of water."

"You might need stitches, Kinley," Logan ordered. "Let me check your hand."

Setting a glass of water on the table beside her, Dan could tell she hated having this attention focused on her because of a mistake on her part. Once again, self-confessed perfectionist Kinley was not in full charge of the situation, and she didn't like that. While he was sure her determination was an asset when it came to work, both in getting the inn off the ground and in her supplemental real-estate career, this was a woman who needed to learn to relax occasionally.

"It doesn't need stitches," Kinley insisted. "It's only a nick."

"It's a little more than a nick," Logan corrected, carefully examining the still-bleeding cut on her left index finger. "But I think you're right that you can skip the stitches. You can probably get by with a bandage for a few days."

"Here's the kit." Bonnie set a white plastic box marked with a red cross on the table. "There's ointment in the box along with adhesive bandages, or gauze and tape if that would be better."

"It'll be fine," Kinley muttered. "I'm sorry I caused such a fuss."

Dan quietly cleaned up the kitchen counter while Logan tended to his sister. He scrubbed a couple drops of blood from the counter and floor, then handed the plastic cutting board to Bonnie, who rinsed it with hot water then placed it in the dishwasher. Kinley had reacted quickly by wrapping her hand with the towel, so she hadn't made much of a mess.

"Thanks, everyone," Kinley said when Logan closed

the first-aid box. "Now if I haven't ruined everyone's appetite, could we just eat and forget about this?"

Dan grinned as he took the seat Bonnie indicated for him. "Very little spoils my appetite. Especially when the food looks and smells as good as this."

Bonnie smiled. "It's just a pot roast and vegetables I cooked in the slow cooker. I made peach cobbler for dessert."

"Bonnie bakes the yeast rolls herself, too," Kinley pointed out, visibly relieved to change the subject from her accident. "She makes a lot of them at a time and stores them in the freezer."

"It all looks delicious. Even the salad," he added with a wink at Kinley that earned him an automatic nose wrinkle.

"Have you enjoyed your first day with us, Dan?" Bonnie asked as they passed the food family-style.

"Very much. Kinley answered a lot of questions for me this morning, and I was able to see some of the area this afternoon. Oh, and we had an excellent lunch at the café, where I met Mary, who seemed very friendly."

Bonnie laughed. "Mary's a hoot. She always has something funny to say."

Maybe he just wanted to see Kinley's reaction when he said lightly to her siblings, "Mary told me about the ghost of Bride Mountain. That was the first I'd heard of the legend."

Right on cue, that little frown appeared between Kinley's brows. Logan made a sound somewhere between a snort and a scoff, making his opinion of the legend clear enough. Only Bonnie smiled in response to the mention.

"It is a rather obscure story," she admitted. "Not a lot of people have heard of it. Maybe we wouldn't have, either, if Uncle Leo and Aunt Helen hadn't seen her and told us about her."

Dan cocked his head at her and spoke without judgment, merely open curiosity. "So you really believe your uncle saw a ghost bride on the night he proposed to his future wife?"

Frowning at her groaning siblings, Bonnie nodded firmly. "I do. I can't explain exactly what they saw, of course, and I'm not saying definitively that I believe in ghosts, but they both spotted something that looked to them like a smiling woman in white. It was a profound experience for both of them, and they were happily married until they were parted by Aunt Helen's death."

"And what about you two?" he asked, including both Kinley and Logan in the question. "No doubt at all on your parts that they were mistaken in what they thought they saw?"

Bonnie answered for them. "Logan thinks it's all malarkey, and Kinley has no whimsy."

Dan was the only one who laughed.

"Where could I learn more about the bride?" he asked. "Do you know of any other couples still living who claim to have seen her?"

Kinley set down her fork abruptly with a slight clatter. "You said you weren't going to write about the bride," she accused him. "You said you're doing a story about wedding venues, not old ghost stories."

"I said I would mention it only within the context of the article I've been employed to write," he replied steadily. "Not a ghost story, but a profile of the historic inn as a Southern wedding venue with its own legends and history attached. But I am curious, naturally, and

I'm not ruling out that it could be a topic of a future article I might write."

They frowned at each other for a moment in a silent battle of wills that Bonnie quickly interrupted. "I do know someone you can talk to," she said to Dan, giving her sister a quick, seemingly uncharacteristically defiant glance. "Her name is Mamie Sawyer and she says she and her late husband saw the ghost. Several people we know claim to have seen her, but Mamie is the only one I would consider really credible. Neither Logan nor Kinley would say a word against her integrity, even if they don't believe in the ghost bride."

Logan chewed on a bite of roast beef, his silence an implicit agreement.

Kinley cleared her throat. "Okay, Mamie would be considered a reliable witness in any court case," she conceded. "That doesn't mean she wasn't mistaken in what she thought she saw forty some–odd years ago."

"I'm sure she'd be happy to visit with you, if you'd like me to set it up, Dan. She's very sociable."

Dan nodded in response to Bonnie's offer, even though he could almost feel the waves of disapproval coming from Kinley. "I'd like that. Thanks."

"I'll let you know after I talk to her. Now, who wants peach cobbler?"

Kinley was rather relieved to make it through dinner without spilling anything on herself, stabbing herself or anyone else with a fork or having her chair collapse beneath her. Considering the way her day had gone thus far, none of the above would have particularly surprised her.

Fortunately, she completed the meal without incident, though she had to excuse herself twice to take business phone calls. The home buyers had made a final offer, which the sellers eventually asked to consider overnight.

Logan hadn't said much during dinner, but he'd been polite enough to their guest to satisfy both her and Bonnie. Their brother wasn't usually rude, he was simply reserved. When the conversation during dessert centered around future plans for the grounds, including the construction of the Meditation Garden and the possibility of purchasing a few adjoining acres for honeymoon cottages, he contributed his share to the subject, outlining plans, discussing options, wryly shooting down what he considered over-the-top suggestions from his enthusiastic and ambitious sisters. Saying he had some computer work to do that evening, he excused himself and left almost immediately after finishing his cobbler.

Dan insisted on helping with cleanup after the meal. He wouldn't allow Kinley to do much more than carry a couple of dishes, telling her he wanted to make sure she kept her bandage dry at least until there was no more risk of bleeding. She was still embarrassed that she'd been so careless. True enough, she didn't have her sister's culinary talents, but she could usually chop a tomato for a salad, for Pete's sake! She should have paid more attention to her task than to Dan's conversation with her sister.

"I'm going to do some prep work for tomorrow's breakfast, then join the guests in the parlor for an hour or so," Bonnie said when the kitchen was spotless again. "I'm sure there will be some games if the two of you would like to participate."

"It sounds like fun," Dan said, "and I do want to visit

with the other guests this evening. But first I think I'll take a walk in the garden."

Surreptitiously flexing her sore hand, Kinley considered whether she should stay for a while longer that evening and discreetly ensure Dan saw the social hour at its best. But because she was confident Bonnie would take care of that, she said, instead, "I'm going to pass on the games tonight. I have a little more work to do this evening. I'll see you tomorrow, Bon. Thanks for dinner, it was great. Sorry I almost ruined the salad."

Laughing, Bonnie gave her a quick hug. "You didn't ruin the salad, just a quarter of a tomato. We got by without it. Take care of that cut."

"I will. Good night."

She and Dan walked outside together. The air had cooled a little as the sun set. She pulled her three-quarter-sleeve cardigan a bit closer around her.

"Are you too cold?" Dan asked, noting the gesture.

She shook her head. "No. It's nice out, isn't it?"

"Very. Will you walk with me for a little while?"

Thinking of the list of things she had to do before bedtime, she hesitated only a moment before shrugging lightly. "I can take a few more minutes."

He looked pleased when he motioned toward the garden path.

Despite the nip in the air, it really was a pleasant evening for a walk. The moon was almost full, glowing softly in the darkening sky. Stars blinked into sight around it. Having spent a fair amount of time in bigger cities, Kinley appreciated being able to see stars here on the mountain. The lighting in the gardens was muted, illuminating the pathways but not so bright as to be intrusive. She and her siblings had put a lot of discussion into the balance between safety and aesthetics, and she hoped they'd reached a satisfactory compromise.

She walked often in the gardens at night, enjoying the sounds of frogs and insects and the occasional hoot of an owl from the woods, underscored by the steady, musical splashing of the central fountain. Bonnie had wanted to install wind chimes, but Logan had vehemently vetoed that request. He hated wind chimes. It was not at all uncommon to cross paths with several guests of the inn enjoying a nighttime stroll, but no one else seemed to be out at the moment, giving a sense of privacy to her walk with Dan. Light spilled from the windows of the inn, both upstairs and down, but few sounds escaped into the quiet night.

Dan kept his voice low, perhaps to avoid disturbing the peaceful ambiance. "Do you ever host nighttime weddings here?"

"Oh, yes, especially in the fall when it starts getting darker earlier but it's still warm enough for comfort. We string fairy lights and use torches and lanterns for illumination. A couple of my favorite weddings here have been after dark."

"Whose idea was it to focus on weddings? The inn was more of a vacation retreat when your great-aunt and great-uncle ran it, wasn't it?"

"It was, though even then quite a few weddings were held here. It was actually my idea to coordinate with other local businesses and specialize in turnkey wedding services," she admitted. "I met with several local florists and caterers and wedding planners and arranged for a couple of magistrates to be on tap if the couples didn't have a specific officiate in mind. Together we came up with the various packages we offer. So far, it's worked out quite well."

"It's got to be a challenge coordinating with all those subcontractors."

She nodded. "As I've mentioned, I enjoy a challenge. And I'm very careful about who I do business with."

He murmured something that sounded like, "No surprise." Maybe he was getting to know her a bit. And maybe, she thought with a slight wince, that would make him less likely to keep flirting with her.

He wouldn't be the first man turned away by what they perceived as her overly controlling nature. She acknowledged that she liked things to be just so, that she thought it her duty to make sure her clients got the best service she could provide for them, that she didn't like being seen as less than competent and efficient—but she hoped secretly that she wasn't quite as pushy and bossy as Eva Sossaman. Like the discussions about safety and beauty with the lighting, she was aware that balance made all the difference.

"Do you have plans for tomorrow?" she asked politely.

"Just hanging out. Checking out the scenery. Taking a few pictures. I could pretty much complete the article tonight, except for the photos from the wedding Saturday."

Was that just the faintest hint of ennui she heard in his voice? Was he somewhat bored by the prospect of writing another fluffy travel profile?

"How long have you been writing for the magazine?" she asked. She knew he was the one who was supposed to be asking the questions, but she was growing increasingly curious about him.

"A little over two years now. Writing for the magazine has given me a chance to travel all over the South, in addition to pursuing some independent projects. I've enjoyed it."

She was pretty sure she heard more than a hint of past tense in that phrasing. Perhaps he was considering a career change soon. Perhaps that book he'd mentioned to Bonnie. "You said you attended the University of Alabama. Did you major in history?"

"No, journalism. History was my minor."

"Have you been writing since?"

"For the most part. I did a four-year hitch in the marines, worked as a foreign correspondent for a couple years in the Middle East, spent some time in London and New York, then let my cousin talk me into working for her. Her magazine was in a state of transition and she thought I could help out. It's worked out pretty well for both of us so far."

Except for the latter part, everything he'd just told her was a complete surprise to her. "You were a marine?"

He nodded, speaking self-deprecatingly. "I spent a lot of time sitting at a desk writing communiqués and press releases from Riyadh. I saw more action as an AP correspondent than I did in the service."

Kinley's mental image of Dan had undergone so many changes that day that she felt a little dizzy now. Expecting a bow-tied older fellow, she'd been startled enough to see a good-looking man in his early thirties with longish hair and a killer smile. Then she'd decided he was a bit of a slacker, a compulsive flirt who seemed to have his job because of his family connections. Now there was this new information that didn't align with any of her preconceptions. Just who was he, anyway?

"You've had a lot of jobs," she said somewhat lamely.

"I guess you could say I have a short attention span," he remarked, which made her swallow hard. If she'd needed more evidence that she shouldn't take his flirting too seriously, he'd just offered it to her.

Keep the conversation light, she reminded herself. Friendly. "You went from working as a foreign correspondent to writing travel articles for a small, regional magazine. Quite a change, wasn't it?"

"Quite a step down, you mean?" he asked, raising an eyebrow as he studied her.

She felt as though she was being tested in some manner, and she didn't like the feeling. She certainly wasn't judging his choice of career. She was simply curious about why he'd made such a drastic change. "I'm sure you had your reasons for accepting your cousin's offer," she said somewhat stiffly.

"I did." But he didn't offer an explanation. Not that he owed her one, of course.

"So, what's next?" she couldn't resist asking. "Planning to move into management at the magazine or focus on that book idea?"

"Management doesn't interest me. I have some other projects I'm considering. Nothing definite at the moment, though whatever I do, I'm sure I'll still be writing. That's my real passion."

Interesting. She would like to hear all about Dan's, um, passions, she thought, clearing her throat. She should probably change the subject—after all, none of this was any of her business—but she couldn't resist trying to learn just a bit more about him. "Do your parents still live in Alabama?"

"Yes. They live in Hoover, not far from my cousin's place."

She remembered his hint that his parents weren't particularly proud of him. At least, that was the way she'd interpreted his ambiguous comment at the café. Was it because of the restless spirit he'd alluded to? If so, how sad that he didn't feel as if he had his parents' support. No matter what they'd endeavored, she and her siblings had always had the security of knowing they had their mother's and each other's full encouragement, even if their father had been conspicuously absent. "How do they feel about your globe-trotting?"

"My parents haven't been pleased with any of my choices since I hit my teens," he answered drily.

She frowned, sensing old resentment in his words, despite his attempt at a joking tone. "Then they must be very hard to please," she said quietly.

He sighed. "They are. In a nutshell, my parents never particularly wanted kids. They hired a series of nannies to raise me after they had me, then they wanted me to fall in line and do everything they wanted once I was old enough for them to take an interest in me. I'm trying to keep up a relationship of sorts with them, but it still isn't easy. And I'm not even sure why I'm telling you all this. I guess spending time with you and your siblings this evening has made me think about my own very different family."

She bit her lip, not quite sure what to say.

Dan frowned suddenly and looked beyond her. "That's enough about me. Is that a ghost I see over there by the trees?"

She was startled into turning to look.

He laughed. "You had to check, didn't you? Maybe you put more credence in the old legend than you think."

She frowned at him. Obviously, he wanted to change the subject, but she couldn't say she appreciated the way he'd gone about it. "Very funny."

He chuckled again, then motioned toward a little wrought iron bench near the fountain, a look of question on his shadowed face. After only a brief hesitation, she sat on one end, and he took the seat beside her.

As he had earlier that day, he reached out to brush a strand of hair from her face. And just as she had before, she felt a little ripple of electricity radiate from that light contact. Water splashed against the stone fountain, providing a musical score for the singing nightlife. Small spotlights were trained on the cascade, making the water glitter as it fell, causing the shadows to dance on the walkway. The fragrant scents of the garden enveloped the little bench, enclosing her and Dan in a cozy little bubble. It was too easy to forget that an inn full of people was only a few yards away. Entirely too easy to forget that she'd known this fascinating man on the bench with her for only a few hours.

His voice was a sexy rumble in her ear. "You really have no sense of whimsy, Kinley?"

She cleared her throat, trying to bring herself back to reality. "So I'm told."

He slid his hand very slowly along the line of her jaw, then traced her lower lip with one fingertip. He was free with his touches—yet from Dan, she didn't mind at all. Perhaps because she sensed that all it would take was a signal from her and he would back off immediately. A signal she didn't particularly want to give at the moment.

"Do you agree with that assessment?"

"Pretty much. That's just the way I am. I believe in what I can see and touch—and prove with my ledger sheets," she said in an attempt at a jest, even though her heart was suddenly beating so quickly in response to his light caress that it made her voice emerge a bit breathlessly.

"Not very romantic," Dan chided, his smile gleaming in the shadowy light.

"I guess I'm just not the romantic type."

"No?"

"No," she whispered.

He leaned his head down to hers as he studied her, his smile so close to her mouth that her parted lips longed to taste him. God, she thought dazedly, when was the last time she'd sat beside a man who made her toes curl?

Much, much too long.

She rested her hands on his shoulders, fingers flexing into the muscles there. "I really should go," she said as much to herself as to him. "I have another two or three hours of work to attend to before I get any rest tonight. And I have to be back early in the morning."

"All business."

Though she knew he was teasing, she nodded. "Exactly."

"I'm not at all sure about that," he said, leaning even closer. "Maybe just a little test...."

A tiny sound of startled pleasure escaped her when she leaned in and her lips covered his. She made no effort to draw away. Just a taste, she promised herself. Just this one moment of weakness.

The kiss was as spectacular as she would have expected from him. Skilled, thorough, generous, enthusiastic. Despite the cool night air, his lips were warm, and a little extra heat seemed to radiate through his clothing. Pressed against him, she could feel for herself that he was as strong and fit as he'd looked from a distance. It wasn't hard to imagine how the rest of that warm, solid body might feel against her own… In fact, the pictures swirled rapidly in her head, adding to the slight dizziness she'd been feeling since they'd walked out into the garden together. If she hadn't known better, she'd have sworn her sister had spiked the lemonade.

Dan groaned softly in protest when she drew back, slowly breaking off the kiss. "Already?"

She drew a deep, slightly ragged breath. Maybe later she would regret uncharacteristically giving in to temptation, but it had definitely been nice while it lasted. "Yes. I have to go."

He sighed, but released her without further argument. Still, she couldn't help but be pleased that he looked so very reluctant to do so.

"I'll see you in the morning," he said.

She stood, her knees a little shaky but otherwise reliable. Dan rose with her. She sighed, then frowned up at him.

"That had nothing to do with either of our work," she reminded him. "It was merely an aberration. Blame it on the moonlight."

"It never would have occurred to me that you'd be anything but professional," he assured her, his easy smile returning, though his eyes still seemed to glow in the darkness.

She nodded and made herself turn away. For some reason, she avoided looking at any dark-shadowed corners of the garden. Not that she expected to see anything out of the ordinary there, she assured herself. "Feel free to look in on the activities in the parlor this evening. Bonnie always sets out tea and light snacks for the games. I have a feeling no one will mind if you snap a few photos for your article."

"I'll be sure and ask."

She was already moving toward the inn. "Don't forget we serve breakfast from seven until nine. If you have any special requests, please let Bonnie know this evening."

"So serious again," he teased from behind her. He reached out to catch her arm just as she reached the bottom of the stairs. "I wonder, Kinley. After I've submitted my article, when you don't have to fret about what I'll write, is there any chance you and I could maybe have dinner or something? The real you, not the vice president of marketing."

"That's not my title," she protested automatically, perhaps to give herself a chance to process the request. "And don't you have someplace else to be after you've finished your article?"

"I could make a little extra time."

She glanced up the stairs toward the door to the inn. "You might be disappointed to find out that you've already met the real me," she said. "With the exception of this uncharacteristic episode, you've seen me pretty much as I am. All business, all the time, as someone once described me."

"Someone who hurt you?"

"Someone who knew me," she corrected evenly.

After a moment, he shook his head. "I'm not sure he did."

"I didn't say it was a he."

"You didn't have to."

Uncertain what to say to that, she hesitated. His gaze held hers and for just a moment, she couldn't seem to make herself move away from him. Dan looked away first, releasing her from the odd spell that she—who did not believe in ghosts or magic or whimsy—seemed to have fallen into for the second time that evening. Maybe she was more tired than she had realized.

"Good night, Kinley. I'll see you tomorrow."

Swallowing, she nodded, then turned and walked up the steps with Dan close behind her.

Chapter Five

Even as tired as she'd been, Kinley slept restlessly Thursday night. She told herself it was because she had so much to do in the next couple of days and was having trouble shutting down her thoughts. She didn't want to accept that her sleep was disturbed entirely by thoughts of Dan Phelan, by mental replays of the time she had spent with him that day. The first unexpected glimpse of him. The smiles he'd given her over the lunch table. The way he'd instinctively moved in front of her when Ninja had appeared ahead of them. The way he'd brushed her cheek in the night shadows of the garden. The kiss they had shared by the fountain—a kiss that she had initiated. The way he gazed into her eyes and made her suspect he saw things in her that she'd buried long ago.

As she carefully applied concealer and makeup to hide any evidence of her disturbed sleep, she told herself she must have been working too intensely lately. Maybe she needed to take a couple of mental health days, something she'd been urging her siblings to do for the past month or so.

Now that the inn was starting to show a profit most months, surely they could all relax just a little—though she, for one, always had a bit of difficulty with that concept. It seemed that she was always working, just as she knew Bonnie and Logan were. None of them had much, if any, social life these days. They should do something to correct that. Not that she saw any future for herself with Dan, of course, but the fact that she had overreacted so much to his flirting was probably an indication that she'd been neglecting that part of her life. How else could she explain the fact that she had planted a kiss on the man the very same day she had met him? she asked herself with a groan.

Because she was awake early, anyway, she arrived at the inn ten minutes before breakfast service began. She had chosen her clothing carefully for the day's events, donning a sleeveless shift dress in bright coral with a narrow cream belt, another three-quarter-sleeve cardigan—this one cream—and a comfortable pair of beige shoes. A discreet flesh-colored bandage covered the healing cut on her index finger.

She'd spent the short drive from her house steeling herself for seeing Dan again, assuring herself she could stay professional today. She'd never really given him an answer about whether she would see him for dinner after his assignment ended, but maybe it was best that she'd waited on that. As tempted as she was to agree, it was always possible that one or both of them could rethink the invitation after spending another day or two together.

She was relieved to see Rhoda had arrived on time that morning, and without destroying more of the inn. Logan and his crew hadn't yet painted the post, other than the initial coat of flat white primer, but already the front looked much better than it had the morning before. The mouthwatering scents of coffee, warm cinnamon and maple syrup greeted her when she walked into the dining room where Bonnie and Rhoda were setting up for breakfast service. Baked cinnamon French toast was today's breakfast casserole offering, with fruit compote and the usual assortment of pastries, hot or cold cereals and yogurt. Her mouth watered in anticipation when she helped herself to a steaming cup of coffee.

"Looks great," she told her sister, who was lighting votive candles in glass holders tucked among arrangements of fresh white roses. Kinley was known as the family perfectionist, but she thought Bonnie was just as concerned with detail, paying careful attention to every aspect of her hostess duties.

Bonnie smiled with a flash of dimples. "Thanks. I promised Serena I'd keep pastries out for an extra couple of hours for her arriving guests."

Kinley plucked a fat strawberry from a bowl and popped it into her mouth. "I'll start calling subcontractors as soon as I've finished breakfast," she said after swallowing. "Just to make sure everything's on track for this evening and tomorrow."

Bonnie nodded absently while running an eye over the dining room to check for any last-minute adjustments. "I wouldn't be surprised if Eva's already started calling them."

Kinley winced. Eva had already fired a photographer and alienated several local vendors. Serena had finally forbidden her mother to make any more calls, insisting she allow Kinley and Bonnie to handle the details, but it would surprise no one if Eva reneged on that agreement. Thirty-six more hours, give or take an hour or two, and this wedding would be over, Kinley reminded herself with a bracing inhale. There could be a permanent hole in her tongue from where she'd bitten it to keep herself from telling Eva exactly what she thought of her at times, but she was determined to get through the remainder of this arrangement without conflict. She wanted good reviews from both Serena and Eva after the wedding.

She sipped her coffee, then asked, "How did things go here last night? Did anyone show up for game night?"

Bonnie turned to walk into the kitchen and Kinley followed. "Oh, yes, almost everyone," Bonnie said over her shoulder. She opened the refrigerator to take out a pitcher of fresh-squeezed orange juice. "The Mayberrys and Travis and Gordon played Scrabble while Dan and I played as Spades partners against that nice couple that checked in yesterday afternoon, the Zakrzewskis. We had a lovely evening."

"Did you?" Kinley frowned into her coffee cup.

"Yes. Dan's quite the card player."

Had Dan flirted with Bonnie? Maybe hinted to her, too, about having dinner sometime? Was that the real game he played?

"It was rather funny how many times he found a reason to casually bring up your name," Bonnie added teasingly. "I think you've made a conquest, Kinley."

Kinley forced a chuckle and spoke lightly to prove

she wasn't taking her sister—or Dan—too seriously. "He's only going to be here for another couple of days. I'm much too busy right now for anything but work. We have that meeting with the new prospective bride this afternoon, the rehearsal and dinner this evening, the wedding tomorrow—not to mention I've got a real-estate deal to attend to later this morning."

"All you ever do is work," Bonnie chided, shaking her head in disapproval.

Kinley cocked an eyebrow. "Said the pot to the kettle. Who's the one who actually lives at the inn 24/7, hmm?"

Bonnie laughed ruefully. "Well, there is that, but at least I'd be open to an evening out with a good-looking single guy if one were to ask. This particular good-looking guy just happens to be more interested in you."

"And just how do you plan to meet a good-looking single guy when you hardly ever leave the inn?" Kinley retorted, ignoring the anything-but-subtle teasing about Dan. "You're the one who should get out more, Bon."

It actually surprised her a little when her sister nodded. "You're right. I should. I have no regrets at all about the two years we've dedicated almost exclusively to this place, but maybe I need to expand my horizons now. I haven't been on more than a handful of dates since we moved here. I should remedy that."

"Yes. Yes, you should. In fact, I know a few—"

Bonnie cut her off with a quick, "Don't even think about it. I am not commissioning you to set me up with anyone, Kinley. When it comes to my love life, you are not in control. Got it?"

"You have a love life?" Rhoda asked quizzically, entering from the laundry room with an armload of clean kitchen towels just in time to hear Bonnie's ultimatum.

"First I've heard of it. Far as I knew, both you girls could use a little nudge in that direction."

With a little growl, Bonnie picked up the orange juice pitcher. "It's time to start the breakfast service. We'll worry about our love lives—or lack thereof—later, shall we?"

That sounded like a very good suggestion to Kinley, who didn't really want her own so-called love life examined too closely at the moment. Just thinking about that reckless kiss in the garden last night made her skin warm uncomfortably, a fact she tried to hide from her sister's too-perceptive eyes.

She moved into the dining room to greet guests as they entered for breakfast, some bright-eyed and eager, others a bit sleepy-lidded and heading straight for the coffee.

"Gordon and I will be checking out right after breakfast," Travis told her regretfully. "We've had a wonderful time, Kinley. We'll definitely be back in the future."

"It's been a pleasure to meet you both," she assured him warmly. "You'd be welcome back anytime."

She paused by the small table where the honeymooning Mayberrys were dining and exchanged some cheery small talk with them before moving on. When she turned again, Dan stood in front of her with a well-filled plate in one hand and a cup of coffee in the other.

She felt her smile twitch a bit, but hoped she managed to mask the reaction by greeting him brightly. "Good morning, Dan."

"Good morning." He nodded toward the coffee cup in her hand. "Have you eaten already?"

"No, not yet."

"Will you join me?"

Aware of the surreptitious attention they were getting from the other diners, she couldn't think of a gracious way to decline. "Just let me get a plate."

Bonnie was refilling the coffee carafe when Kinley filled her plate. "Having breakfast with Dan, hmm?" Bonnie teased in a murmur. "So maybe you listened to me, after all?"

Kinley gave her sister a look, then turned with her plate to cross the room to the window-side table Dan had chosen.

Dan nodded a bit sheepishly toward the generous helpings of food on his plate. "For someone trained in the management part of the hospitality business, your sister is an excellent chef."

Cutting into her own smaller serving, Kinley agreed. "She trained in that, too. Bonnie's prepared for this since she was a child. She used to play hotel with her dolls and stuffed animals. She checked them in, then fed them and suggested interesting things for them to do to entertain themselves. And then she cleaned their rooms."

Dan laughed. "Seriously?"

"She made the rooms out of cardboard boxes, decorated them and stacked them like a hotel with the front wall sliced off. She used to charge me a nickel to let my dolls spend the night in her inn. She was five then; I was eight."

"That's really funny."

"Is it any wonder she was Uncle Leo's favorite? Every time we came to visit she tagged at his heels asking a million questions about running the inn."

"And about the ghost?"

Kinley paused only a moment in her eating, then

swallowed and reached for her coffee. She really wished Dan would forget all about the ghost. "He didn't tell her about that until she was older. He said he was concerned that hearing about a ghost would make her nervous about staying here. Bonnie thought the real reason was because he couldn't bear to think about that night for a long time after Aunt Helen died because it made him too sad."

"What about your brother?" Dan asked, picking up her signals and obligingly changing the subject. "Did he bring his toys to Bonnie's hotel?"

"No, he was much too cool for that," she quipped, grateful for the diversion. "He's almost two years older than I am. Even as a kid he was obsessed with computers and blueprints and that sort of thing. He designed a handicap-accessible playground for our church with a desktop computer and a CAD program when he was only fourteen years old."

"Impressive."

"He is."

"It was obvious during dinner last night that you and Bonnie are both crazy about your brother, even though you both seem to get frustrated with him fairly often."

"I'd say those are both accurate assessments," she agreed with a faint smile. Every time she thought of their brother's devastating illness in his early twenties, her chest tightened. She wouldn't mention that painful year to Dan now—Logan wouldn't want her talking about it—but she didn't try to hide the affection that underlay her frequent exasperation with her big brother.

"I enjoyed meeting with him," Dan said, "but he's a bit hard to get to know, I think. Very reserved."

"That's accurate, too. Our brother is a great guy, but

he's had some serious challenges to overcome. That's left him a little grouchy, but Bonnie and I are working on that."

She could tell he was curious about the challenges she'd mentioned, but he didn't follow up, saying merely, "It's nice that the three of you are so close."

Once again, she had a funny suspicion that he was comparing his own family to hers and that his came up short. Though he'd spoken rather lightly about his parents' disapproval, she'd sensed the old pain in his voice. He'd said his parents hadn't approved of him since his teens. It had been a throwaway line, but something in his tone had made her believe there was at least some truth to his words. She had spent almost all day with him yesterday, so in some ways it felt as though she'd gotten to know him rather quickly, but of course there was still much about him she didn't know. And she couldn't help being increasingly curious.

"What's on your schedule for today?" he asked, interrupting her musings.

"I have a busy day planned getting ready for the wedding rehearsal and dinner this evening. This afternoon I have a meeting with a prospective bride and then a phone conference with a supplier. And I'm expecting another counteroffer from the sellers of the house deal I was working last night."

"So just a typical day for Kinley," he said over his coffee cup.

She nodded. "Pretty much. I had originally planned to give you the grand tour and answer questions this morning, but we got that out of the way yesterday. You'd be welcome to tag along with me today and observe some of the behind-the-scenes preparation for a wedding, if you wouldn't find that too boring. Or I can direct you to some more of the local attractions, which might be more fun for you. It's going to be a beautiful day for sightseeing."

"I can't imagine I'd get bored spending the day with you."

It was the first time that morning he'd openly flirted with her again. And her little jolt of reaction reminded her that she liked it. Realizing she was sitting there gazing at his sexy mouth—and remembering too vividly how it felt pressed to hers—she snapped out of it and said briskly, "I wouldn't be so sure about that. It's going to be a long, detail-filled day. Feel free to cut out whenever you get restless, and let us know if we can give you any assistance."

"And now she's back in hostess mode," he murmured teasingly, earning himself a look that only made him laugh.

They were almost finished with breakfast when Eva Sossaman swept into the dining room with Serena and young Grayson. Eva and her husband lived only a twenty-minute drive from the inn, close enough that there was no need for them to stay overnight, and Serena was living with them, leaving the inn's limited accommodations free for their out-of-town guests. The boy made a beeline straight for the buffet table, though he had undoubtedly already been fed breakfast at his grandmother's house.

"Don't touch anything, Grayson," Eva said automatically, then immediately turned away to leave Bonnie to protect the food. Bonnie sat the boy at a table with a small pastry and a glass of juice, then hovered nearby to make sure he stayed there.

Eva homed in directly on Kinley and Dan. She sashayed toward them, her sparkly clothes fluttering around her. She'd definitely dressed to impress today, Kinley thought wryly. Her hair was sprayed into an ash-blond helmet of curls, and diamonds flashed from her ears and fingers. There was no doubt she'd dressed with cameras in mind. Serena, on the other hand, had chosen a more conservative outfit, a cap-sleeve knit dress in a muted beige color that was a bit too close to her skin tone, making her look somewhat washed out. She'd left her brown hair loose, and wore little makeup. Kinley thought she looked tired.

"I was happy to see that young man was starting to paint the new post when we arrived," Eva announced. "I pointed out a few places he needed to be sure not to miss, but it already looks much better than it did yesterday. Serena and I are greatly relieved."

"Mom, Kinley and Mr. Phelan are having breakfast," Serena murmured, tugging at her mother's arm. "Why don't you wait until they're finished?"

"It's okay, Serena, I'm finished." Kinley gave Dan a quick, apologetic look, then rose. She gathered her dishes to carry to the table designated for that purpose; Rhoda would collect them later and stack them in the dishwasher. Dan followed with his.

"I want another one," Grayson called out loudly, pointing toward the glass-dome-covered tray of pastries.

"You've had enough, Grayson," his grandmother replied firmly, setting off high-pitched whining that made Kinley's ears ring.

"He's going to be bored out of his mind today," Serena muttered. "There really was no need for us to be here so early, Mom."

"Now, Serena, you want to make sure everything is just perfect for your rehearsal this evening and for the wedding tomorrow."

"No, Mother, *you* want to make sure of that," her daughter snapped.

Kinley moved quickly to intercede. In the months she'd been working with them, she had seen Serena stand up to her mother only rarely, and Eva never reacted well. "I can understand why you both want to keep an eye on things, but there isn't a lot you can do for now. Bonnie and Rhoda have the rooms ready for your guests, Logan and his crew are setting up outside. As soon as breakfast service is cleared away, Bonnie and Rhoda will start getting the dining room ready for the rehearsal dinner. So, really, everything is under control here."

"See, Mom? It's all under control," Serena repeated. "We should leave them to their work and go take care of our own list of things to do today. Connor and Alicia are supposed to meet us at our house this afternoon, remember, so we can all arrive for the rehearsal together. Grayson will be happy to see his mom and dad again after almost a week. So let's just go, okay?"

"Yes, we will," her mother said with a dismissive wave of her hand. "But first I want to go out and check on the progress around the gazebo. I'll just have a word with Logan and make sure—"

"I think it would be much better if you let me check with my brother," Kinley suggested quickly. "He can get a little, um, curt when he's focused on a project, and he'll be directing his entire attention to getting ready for the wedding, I assure you."

Dan inched forward, drawing attention to himself with a diffident smile. "Actually, Mrs. Sossaman, I wonder if you and your lovely daughter could spare a minute to chat with me this morning. We haven't had a chance to talk for the article I'm writing. I'd love to have your input—you know, why you chose the inn as a setting for the wedding, any advice you might have to offer other future brides. That sort of thing."

He was totally playing her, of course, but Eva was either too oblivious or too vain to care. Her attention immediately diverted from the activities outside, she graciously consented to an interview with Dan, assuring him she had quite a few valuable suggestions to offer to prospective brides. Serena rolled her eyes, but looked relieved that yet another confrontation had been avoided.

"I'm so sorry," she murmured to Kinley, hanging back for a moment when Dan walked toward the parlor with Eva and Grayson—who had been slightly mollified with a handful of grapes from Bonnie. "I'm sure you'll be very glad when this wedding is over and you won't have to deal with my mother anymore."

"Your mother simply wants her only daughter's wedding to be perfect," Kinley replied with a faint smile. "That's understandable."

Serena pushed a hand through her hair and scowled. "Well, she's driving me crazy. Not to mention poor Chris. He's been avoiding me for the past week just so he doesn't have to deal with my mother haranguing him about all the details the groom and his family are supposed to be responsible for. I keep telling her to just let them take care of things their way, but she never listens."

Resting a soothing hand on the younger woman's shoulder, Kinley said, "Trust me, Serena, I've seen plenty of family meltdowns during the last hours before a wedding. People just get overwhelmed by what they perceive to be an overabundance of details to take care of. They start thinking of everything that could go wrong, and they end up snapping at the ones closest to them. Just relax and try to enjoy this special time. Let us deal with the worries, okay? I'm sure there will be a couple of minor mishaps, but usually those just give you something to laugh about in years to come, you know?"

Drawing a deep, ragged breath, Serena pushed back her hair again and nodded. "Thanks, Kinley. I'll try to hold on to my patience with her."

"That would be best." She was making a massive effort to do the same.

Serena relaxed enough to give just a slight smile. "Thank goodness for your friend. Mom will be less likely to cause any problems in front of him, although she'll certainly put on airs for him."

"My, um—"

"He seems very nice," Serena added, glancing in the direction of the parlor. "Have you known him long?"

"I met him yesterday for the first time. He's here on assignment for the magazine for a series of articles profiling small Southern wedding venues."

"Really? You only met him yesterday?" Serena looked surprised.

"Yes." Kinley, too, found it a bit hard to believe, especially when she thought of that interlude in the garden last night.

"Huh. I'd have thought you knew each other longer. Something about the way he smiles at you, I guess."

"Serena!" Eva called from the hallway. "Are you coming? Dan wants to talk to you, too. After all, you are the bride."

"Glad she remembers that occasionally," Serena muttered, but obligingly headed in the direction of her mother's voice. "Let me know if you need anything from me today, Kinley," she said over her shoulder.

"Same to you. You have my number." Ordering herself to concentrate solely on business for now, Kinley hurried toward the office to start making her calls, leaving Bonnie and Rhoda to clear away the now-emptied dining room.

It was inevitable, of course, that some things would go wrong that day. Kinley pretty much planned for unexpected problems so she would be prepared to deal with whatever cropped up. She hoped she could take care of whatever she encountered quickly and discreetly, as she always tried to do, but especially with Dan there.

Dan was able to keep Eva occupied for almost an hour, during which Kinley accomplished quite a bit. He caught up with her later that morning back in the dining room, where she was helping Rhoda and Bonnie set up tables for the rehearsal dinner that evening. By moving the four usual tables closer together and bringing down another round folding table and six more chairs from the attic, they had provided seating for thirty, plus a kids' table that would hold six. Dan jumped in to help when he saw Bonnie carrying two chairs, taking them from her and placing them where she indicated.

Having just set the smaller chairs in place at the

kids' table, Kinley brushed off her hands absently as she looked at Dan. "Well? How did it go?"

He smiled and shrugged. "Let's just say I have much more information on tomorrow's wedding than I'll need to use in the article. Not to mention the life story of both the bride and the groom, and the bride's mother's role in bringing them together."

Kinley grimaced apologetically. "I'm really sorry about that."

He shrugged. "All part of the job. How's it going with you?"

"Great," she said brightly, pushing out of her mind any thoughts of vendor delays, miscommunications and other issues she'd dealt with in the past hour. "Did Serena and Eva leave?"

"I walked them to the door. I hope they went straight to their car from there, which is what Serena was strongly urging they do. By the way, you might want to send someone in to tidy the parlor. Young Grayson is very, um, curious. Not to mention energetic."

"Thanks. I'll take care of that."

"Is there anything I can do to help?"

"Oh, no, thanks. Everything's under control. Maybe you'd like to—"

"Kinley." Logan appeared in the doorway to the deck, which had been left open to keep the fresh air circulating in the room. "Keep her away from me, will you?"

Wincing, Kinley hurried to her brother. She didn't have to ask who he meant by her, of course. "What happened?"

"She came back giving orders to my crew, telling me

what I was doing wrong—nothing, by the way. Telling me better ways of doing my job—which weren't better."

"Where is she?"

"She left. Her daughter burst into tears and dragged her away."

Kinley put a hand to her head. "You made Serena cry?"

Logan snorted in offense. "I did not. Her mother made her cry. I just told them I knew what I was doing and didn't really need them to supervise."

"Please tell me you were at least reasonably polite about it."

"I know how to do my job," he repeated slowly for her benefit. "I was as polite as I could be. She should just be damned glad I didn't throw something at her."

Still rubbing her temple with one hand, Kinley waved off her brother with the other. "Just go back to work. Maybe she'll stay away for a while now."

"She'd better."

Just as Logan turned and stalked away, Bonnie rushed in from the kitchen. "Kinley, I can't find those place-card holders Eva wanted to use tonight. You did pick them up, right?"

"Yes, of course I did. I put them… Oh, crap." She had a sudden, vividly detailed mental picture of the box of holders. Sitting on the coffee table in her living room. "I left them at home. I'll have to run and get them."

Bonnie glanced at her watch. "You have about an hour and forty-five minutes before the meeting with the prospective clients. You might as well have lunch while you're out, then be back in time for the meeting. Rhoda and I will make sure everything is ready in here for the caterer."

Automatically checking the time on her phone, Kinley nodded. "Yes, that will work. Is there anything else you need me to pick up for you while I'm out?"

"A couple of things. I'll text them to you. Perhaps Dan would like to ride along with you?" Bonnie suggested, her tone guileless.

"I'm sure Dan can find something more fun to do than join me running errands," Kinley prevaricated.

He smiled blandly at her. "Actually, I'd love to join you. Besides," he added in a conspiratorial tone, "I'm afraid Mrs. Sossaman might return while you're gone. There's really nothing left for me to interview her about."

"I'll try to keep her busy if she does return," Bonnie volunteered. "It's my turn, I suppose."

"Just keep her away from Logan."

Bonnie laughed. "I'll certainly try."

Kinley glanced at Dan then. "You're sure you want to come with me?"

"Absolutely," he said without hesitation.

Trying to ignore the little ripple of reaction to his deep voice, she turned and spoke rather too brusquely, aware that she sounded a bit more like her brother than she would have liked. "Well, let's go then. I have a lot to do today."

Dan chuckled and fell into step behind her.

Chapter Six

Kinley's tidy rental house was located on the outskirts of Radford, just a twenty minute drive from the inn in good weather. A simple, white frame one story, it featured a covered stoop on which she'd placed a planter filled with spring flowers, plain black shutters and an open carport.

Rather than pulling all the way into the carport and entering through the kitchen, as she usually did, she parked in the drive and ushered Dan in through the front door. It seemed only polite to invite him in rather than expect him to wait in the car while she retrieved the things Bonnie had requested.

With the landlord's permission, she had painted the inside walls a rich cadet blue with bright white trim. She'd polished the wood floors to a warm gleam. The doorways were arched, and a white brick, gas log fireplace was the focal point of the small living room.

She had three bedrooms, one of which she used as a home office, two baths, a tiny dining room and a sunny kitchen with new appliances and granite countertops. She'd furnished simply with light colors and clean lines to make the best use of her limited space. She didn't intend to stay here forever, but it had been a very comfortable home for her for the past couple of years—not that she spent all that much time here.

"Nice," Dan said with a look around.

"Thanks." She shook her head as she walked to the coffee table on which sat a large box. "There's the box I forgot. Can't believe I walked out without it this morning. I usually go through a mental checklist to make sure I have everything I'm supposed to take with me."

"Maybe you had something else on your mind this morning."

She glanced around to find that he stood very close to her, and that he was studying her with a quirked eyebrow and a half smile. With that particular expression and his longish dark hair breeze-tossed around his face, those jewel-blue eyes gleaming in his tanned face, he looked like the quintessential bad boy—almost impossible to resist, regardless of her better judgment.

"Or someone," she agreed slowly.

The other side of his mouth twitched, tilting up into a full smile. "Eva Sossaman?"

She wrinkled her nose at him. "Very funny."

He brushed his lips over that little wrinkle before saying, "There's something about you, Kinley Carmichael, that makes it very hard for me to remember that I'm supposed to be working. I've never been the strictly business type, as any of my former employers could tell you, but I swear I don't usually forget I'm on assignment every time a pretty woman frowns at me."

She wasn't sure how she felt about his comments. Flattered. Flustered. A little wary. And really? He liked it when she frowned at him?

As if he'd read the thoughts flashing across her face, he laughed. He traced a fingertip in the faint crease between her eyebrows. "You're doing it again. Gets to me every time."

She poked his very close—and very fine—chest with one finger. "I know your type. You, Dan Phelan, are a flirt. A player."

"I'll grant you the first. There's nothing wrong with a little lighthearted flirtation, as long as it doesn't cross the line into offensive. I flirt all the time with my neighbor back home—and she's eighty-three. Gives as good as she takes. She calls me her 'fancy boy,'" he added with a laugh.

"As for the player part—no. Not if you mean someone who uses women and then moves on. That's not who I am. I'm always entirely honest with the women I spend time with, and when I'm in a relationship, it's exclusive. And before you ask, there isn't currently a relationship and there haven't been that many in the past. I've been pretty busy for the past decade or so."

From the brief bio he'd given her, she'd say he had been busy! But why was he telling her these things now?

"What about you, Kinley? You said there isn't anyone at the moment?"

"I was married once, several years ago," she answered evenly. "It didn't last long—just long enough to teach me that I'm much better at business than relationships."

Dan's expressive eyebrow rose again. "You gave up after one painful disappointment?"

"I didn't give up," she corrected him immediately. "I redirected my attention to areas I was stronger in. I, um, don't like to fail," she added in a mutter. "In anything."

"I'd already figured that out about you."

She tossed her head somewhat defiantly. She didn't enjoy openly dissecting her weaknesses, though she would not shy away from admitting them. "Like I said, all business, all the time."

"You were quoting someone else at the time. The ex?"

She shrugged. "Oddly enough, I thought he was focused on career success, too. Everyone, including him, always said we were two of a kind—until he changed his mind eight months after the wedding and decided he'd rather be a carefree bachelor and spend most of his life playing. He said he was sorry, but a wife didn't fit into that unapologetically hedonistic scenario—another direct quote, by the way."

"Wow. Sounds like a real winner."

"Oh, he's still the overachiever he always was," she said with a dry laugh that didn't quite mask the shock she still felt whenever she remembered that out-of-the-blue announcement. "The difference is that now he's determined to be the very best 'party dude' ever. Tom was always one to set his sights high."

Dan reached out to touch her hand. "He did hurt you," he murmured, alluding to their conversation in the garden last night.

It seemed futile to deny it. "Yes. But I got over it."

"I'm not so sure you did." He slid his hand up her arm to lightly tap her shoulder. "There's a little chip here that I suspect wasn't there before. Maybe that need for control you've admitted to has a lot to do with making sure you don't get hurt that way again."

"I told you," she said with a swallow. "I don't like to fail."

"Sounds to me like you're taking too much credit for that particular failure."

She moistened her lips and shrugged. "Maybe."

Which didn't mean she wouldn't do everything in her power to minimize the odds of such failures in the future, she added silently.

Dan looked thoughtful as he digested the glimpses she'd given him of her past. "I do think there should be a balance between all work and all play."

The faintest of sighs escaped her. She pushed the painful memories to the back of her mind where she usually kept them and admitted, "I've always had trouble with that balance thing, myself."

Lowering his head, he spoke almost against her lips. "Maybe you could use a little help with that."

No, she thought, she didn't need any help balancing her life. She had everything laid out exactly the way she wanted, her career plans clearly outlined, short-term goals defined and satisfactorily underway. She'd tried the marriage thing, and it hadn't paid off for her, but she hadn't totally ruled out the occasional light-hearted fling. As long as both parties knew from the start that it wasn't serious, that she wouldn't allow herself to be derailed again from her long-term plans. Since she doubted that footloose Dan Phelan was any more interested in being tied down than she was, maybe there would be no harm in enjoying his attentions during the brief time he would be around.

Giving in to temptation, she rose the half inch needed to bring their lips together. Dan gathered her into his arms, and for the first time she was pressed fully against that fit body, keenly aware of every ridge of muscle, every strong angle—and the unmistakable evidence that their kisses were as arousing to him as they were to her.

She could almost feel her insides melt with hunger for him. It had been much, much too long since she'd wanted anyone this much, since any man's smile had turned her knees to jelly, since anyone's kiss had cleared her mind of every thought but of him. Actually, she didn't think she'd ever reacted to anyone quite the same way she had to Dan—certainly not as fast.

She slid her hands up his chest, around his neck. Buried her fingers in the back of his lush, dark hair. His hands glided down her back, shaping her curves, holding her more tightly against him. Instinctively, she shifted her weight, moving against him in a way that made a low groan rumble in his chest. She felt his fingers tighten at her hips, which only made her long to feel his hands on every inch of her.

He took his time exploring her mouth. Nibbling her lower lip, tracing it with just the tip of his tongue, taking teasing little nips until she moaned in frustration and tugged at the back of his head in demand of more. His chuckle was muffled when their mouths fused, and then changed to a soft groan when their tongues met in a demanding duel. Teasing turned to craving, light touches became more frantic.

For a moment, she thought the sudden vibration she felt was coming from her overstimulated nerve endings. That her ears were ringing with the force of her fully reawakened desire. She realized rather sheepishly that her phone was chiming in her pocket.

Dan released her reluctantly when she drew back. Blowing out a pent-up breath, he pushed a hand through his hair, giving her a crooked, pained smile as he moved away to give her a little space to answer the call.

She cleared her throat before speaking. "Hi, Bonnie, what's up?" she asked maybe a little too brightly.

"I hope you haven't ordered lunch yet." Her sister's voice held a grim note that made Kinley wince.

"No, why?"

"We have a situation here."

"What's wrong?" She almost hated to ask. She already suspected she knew whose name was about to pop up.

She was right. "Eva called with a last-minute brainstorm." Continuing over Kinley's groan, Bonnie explained, "She's decided she wants big lavender organza bows decorated with white calla lilies on the back of each chair for the rehearsal dinner this evening."

"Did you tell her it's too late to make that sort of request? Not to mention that the rehearsal dinner is the groom's family's responsibility?"

"I tried. She said she checked with the groom's mother, who told her that would be fine. Probably browbeat the poor woman into agreeing. Anyway, Eva said if we don't have time to take care of it, she'll pick up the supplies and come do it herself. She got very insistent. I told her I'd get back with her."

"Damn it." The thought of Eva Sossaman hanging around all afternoon, making a mess of the decorating and insisting everyone else help her, not to mention "supervising" all the other preparations, made Kinley shudder. She didn't even want to think about how long Logan would be able to hold his temper in check, even though he'd shown admirable restraint with Eva thus far. "Tell her we'll handle it. Do we have enough organza?"

"You should probably pick up some extra," Bonnie suggested apologetically. "I've already put in an emergency call to the florist. She'll send over three dozen of those silk calla lilies Eva wanted us to use in the garlands. Fortunately she had extra in stock. She said something told her she'd better be prepared for last-minute requests from Eva."

The whole inn was going to be draped in lavender organza and clusters of white silk calla lilies by the time Eva finished, Kinley thought irritably. Not to mention the real white lilies and lavender sweet peas that would make up centerpieces, bouquets and assorted fresh flower arrangements. Eva had apparently never heard the expression, "Less is more."

"I hope you reminded her that she's adding to her costs by ordering last-minute extras."

"Of course I did. She said not to worry about the expense."

Which was why they'd all managed to hold on to their strained patience with Eva to this point, Kinley reminded herself wryly. She was a pain in the butt, but she was paying very generously for this wedding.

"I'm sorry," she said to Dan when she'd returned her phone to her pocket. "I have to go. I've got to pick up some organza at the crafts store, then head back to the inn to help Bonnie tie bows on the chairs. A last-minute brainstorm on Eva's part."

He chuckled in resignation. "Yeah, I figured that out."

"I'm sorry about lunch."

He shrugged. "I'll find something. I'm not hungry now, anyway. Not for food, at least," he added in a meaningful murmur that made her cheeks warm.

It was just as well, she thought, that Bonnie had called at that moment, before she could do something really stupid. She'd been a kiss and a heartbeat away from dragging Dan to the nearest flat surface. And she was fully aware that he would not have resisted. If she were the type of woman who believed in magic and spells, she might have suspected he'd cast one on her, considering how atypically she had behaved since he'd arrived only yesterday.

"I think I'm in the mood to write this afternoon," he added, sliding his hand down her arm. "Not an article, but the book I've been itching to write. Maybe you're my muse, Kinley."

She smiled faintly. "I've never been called anyone's muse before."

"And I've never met anyone who inspired me so quickly." He brushed one last kiss across her lips before making himself move back.

She reminded herself firmly that he was scheduled to leave tomorrow evening, despite his hints that he wouldn't mind staying a little longer to get to know her better. It would surely be best for all involved if they stuck to the original schedule. Hadn't she just told him, and reminded herself, that she wasn't particularly successful when it came to romance? For someone who hated failure as badly as she did, that meant she should especially avoid getting involved with someone who affected her as strongly as Dan did.

"We should go," she said gruffly, heading for the door. At least she would be too busy the rest of the day to get into further trouble with him. From this moment on, she would focus strictly on business, making no more foolish mistakes.

"Um, Kinley?"

Her hand was already on the door. "Yes?"

"Weren't you going to take this box with you?" He motioned toward the coffee table with barely hidden amusement.

Exhaling impatiently, she nodded and moved toward it, but Dan had already picked up the big box. "I've got it," he said, grinning.

Biting her lip, she turned and walked outside, then waited for him to pass her so she could lock the door behind them.

After helping Kinley carry in the supplies they'd brought, Dan hung around to assist with the frantic changes to the decor. Kinley reminded him that he had planned to write that afternoon, but he seemed in no hurry to return to his room. He appeared to enjoy spending time with her and Bonnie, getting a peek behind the scenes of the wedding preparations. He didn't actually tie bows, laughingly claiming to be all thumbs when it came to that sort of thing, but he cut the required lengths of ribbon and then tucked silk lilies into the loops as Kinley directed, freeing Rhoda and Bonnie to take care of the many other daily details of running the inn and preparing for a wedding.

Setting out cutesy little place cards in the holders

Kinley had retrieved, Bonnie looked up to smile at Dan. "You never imagined you'd spend an hour today playing arts and crafts, did you?"

Handing Kinley the last length of measured ribbon, he smiled. "Well, no. But it's been interesting. I can say now that I've seen the hard work that goes into a wedding."

"You've only seen our part," Bonnie corrected him. "The florist is making bouquets and arrangements, the baker will have many hours invested in decorating the wedding cake and the groom's cake, the caterer has been preparing food for tonight and will provide the meal after the wedding tomorrow, the musicians are practicing, photographer and videographer are coordinating…"

Dan laughed and held up a hand to stop her. "Okay, I get the picture. Weddings are a hell of a lot of trouble and expense."

"They can be," Bonnie agreed, carefully referring to the seating chart as she moved to another table. Kinley knew her sister would check all the tables again when she'd set out all the place cards. Neither of them wanted to deal with Eva's wrath if her painstakingly coordinated seating arrangements weren't exactly as she had specified—even though, as she reiterated piously, the rehearsal dinner was up to the groom's family to manage. "Personally, I'd like a small, simple ceremony if I ever get married. Just family and my closest friends."

"I had two weddings like that," Rhoda said with a reminiscent sigh, carrying an armload of snowy napkins into the room. "One on the beach, one in a mountain meadow. Back in the seventies. First marriage lasted ten years, the second one only two, but the weddings were beautiful."

Dan met Kinley's eyes with a grin. "And how do *you* feel about weddings?"

"We at Bride Mountain Inn strive to provide the most beautiful wedding experience any bride could hope for," she recited almost word for word from their advertising materials. "From simple, intimate ceremonies to luxury affairs for up to 150 guests, we do our best to make a bride's dream wedding come true."

"I'll be sure and quote you on that," he said gravely.

"You do that." She stood back from tying the last jaunty bow to run a critical eye around the room. "Everything's looking good, Bonnie."

"It looks as if it was decorated for a birthday party for a princess-obsessed five-year-old," Rhoda muttered. "But it's exactly what Miz Sossaman wants, I guess."

"Rhoda," Bonnie chided. She and Kinley both had to remind their employee frequently to be tactful and circumspect in front of guests. Rhoda should understand that included the writer who was here to profile the inn.

Kinley glanced at her watch. "I should get ready for my meeting. Cassie Drennan and her fiancé are supposed to be here soon. Bonnie, you know where to find me if you need me. Dan—"

"I think I'll walk down to the café to try that pie Mary bragged about yesterday, and then I'll spend a couple hours writing in my room," he said. "Can I bring you anything?"

"Thanks, but I'll find something in the kitchen after my meeting."

He nodded. "So I'll look you up later."

Not quite meeting his eyes, she nodded.

The office opened off the foyer, behind the reception desk. It wasn't big, but by keeping the furnishings to a minimum they had made the most of the space. Instead of a desk, the room held a conference table surrounded by six chairs, and another chair or two could be pulled in if necessary. Kinley arranged a pitcher of ice water and a fresh carafe of coffee on a low credenza along with water glasses, coffee cups, sugar and cream, then took a seat at one end of the table. She propped her tablet computer in front of her and skimmed through the few notes she'd taken in a preliminary phone call with the future bride who was scheduled to arrive in ten minutes.

Cassie Drennan had sounded young and eager, excited to be making plans for a late-summer wedding. She'd explained she knew three months was a shorter planning period than many brides probably gave themselves, but her fiancé had accepted a position in London and the window of opportunity for their wedding was narrow. She'd been thrilled that the requested August weekend was available for a wedding in the garden of the inn.

"Chris Thompson's dad just dropped off the favors for tonight," Bonnie said, entering the office with a large cardboard box. "Want to see? They're nice."

"Sure."

The stainless steel wine bottle stoppers topped with stainless steel hearts would be laid at each place setting as mementoes of the rehearsal dinner. The bride and groom would have special gifts for each member of their wedding party, but these favors had been provided by the groom's parents.

"They are nice," Kinley said, hefting one of the plastic-bubble-wrapped stoppers in her hand. "I'm sure they'll be appreciated."

"The kids' table will have little silver-plate buckets

of fruit candies wrapped in purple cellophane. Rhoda's setting those out now."

"Maybe we'll actually survive this affair, after all."

Bonnie laughed and pushed a weary hand through her tousled blond hair. "Don't speak too confidently. We still have tonight and tomorrow to get through."

"We'll make it. All we have to do is keep our brother from throttling the mother of the bride," Kinley said in a stage whisper, one eye on the open office doorway.

"Or keep the bride from doing so," Bonnie said in the same low voice, her eyes lit with a rueful smile.

Kinley couldn't help but imagine the humiliated look on Serena Sossaman's face when she'd dragged her mother away that morning. "That, too."

Bonnie toyed with the open lid of the favors box. "I'm sorry I had to cut your lunch outing short. If I'd thought there was time, I'd have waited until you'd had a chance to eat to call you."

"You did the right thing," Kinley said firmly. "There's no way we'd have finished in time if you hadn't."

"I know. But still—it's too bad you didn't get to have lunch with Dan."

Kinley wasn't at all sure she and Dan would have gotten around to having lunch if Bonnie's call hadn't interrupted them—not that she had any intention of admitting that, of course. "We already had this talk, Bon. No matchmaking, remember? I'll stay out of yours, you stay out of mine."

Bonnie gave a little huff of exasperation. "But he's so nice. And so cute. And so obviously taken with you. If you'd just make a little time for him…"

"I don't *have* time," Kinley said, as much to herself

as to her sister. "I'm working two jobs and barely fitting everything in as it is. Maybe his job allows him to just take random days off when he likes, but I don't have that luxury. And you know how long guys usually stay around once they figure out I'm not going to just drop all my responsibilities to cater to them. Not very long at all."

"You do have a knack for running them off," Bonnie agreed with a sister's candor. "I've started to wonder if you push them away to avoid dealing with the risks."

"You know what we *really* don't have time for right now? Amateur analysis." Kinley looked pointedly down at her tablet. Both Bonnie and Dan had now suggested that her divorce had left her afraid of future involvement. They were wrong, of course. The disaster of a marriage had left her more embarrassed than devastated. Perhaps it had reinforced her lifelong aversion to failure, but it hadn't left her brokenhearted.

"You're right," Bonnie conceded grudgingly. "We'll talk later."

But not about Dan, Kinley vowed silently. She needed to come to terms with her own thoughts and feelings about him before she could even begin to discuss him with her sister.

She heard the front door open, heard voices in the entryway, and she stood to greet the arriving guests. Balancing the open favors box in front of her, Bonnie turned to hurry out of the office. She rushed through the open doorway—and straight into a tall, solid man who was approaching from the other direction. The resulting collision sent box and Bonnie tumbling to the floor.

Kinley leaped forward in response to her sister's startled cry. There was a moment of pandemonium as the newcomers gathered around Bonnie, who looked thoroughly embarrassed as she assured everyone she was unharmed. With the help of the apologetic man she'd barreled into, she gathered the scattered bottle stoppers.

"They're fine, Kinley," Bonnie said, still kneeling on the floor as she carefully placed the stoppers back in the box, checking each one for signs of damage. Fortunately, they were all still wrapped in the plastic packing, so there were no scratches from the incident.

Kinley shook her head. "Forget about the stoppers, are you hurt?"

"I'm okay. Really."

"I'm so sorry," the tall man said again, bending to offer Bonnie a hand.

Her smaller hand was swallowed by his. She made a funny little sound, then laughed somewhat breathlessly when he helped her to her feet. "Static electricity," she said. "I got a little shock."

"I felt it, too," he assured her.

Kinley lifted an eyebrow slightly in response to the rather dazed look on her sister's face. Bonnie must have been quite flustered by the accident. Either that, or her reaction to the nice-looking man's touch wasn't all due to static electricity.

"Honestly, Dad." A pretty young woman stepped forward with a teasingly disapproving shake of her strawberry blond head. "I can't take you anywhere."

Dad? Kinley mentally adjusted the man's age up about a decade. She'd have guessed him to be in his early thirties, but his daughter wore a big engagement ring on her left hand and was obviously no child.

Bonnie bent quickly to pick up the box, her face momentarily hidden by her thick blond hair. When she straightened again, she wore a bright smile that gave no clue to her thoughts. "Perhaps we should start over. I'm Bonnie Carmichael, and this is my sister, Kinley. We're the owners of Bride Mountain Inn."

The younger woman spoke again, beaming in Kinley's direction. "Hi, I'm Cassie Drennan. We spoke on the phone?"

"Of course. You're the bride-to-be. It's a pleasure to meet you."

"This clumsy oaf is my dad, Paul Drennan," she teased, patting her father's arm.

Smiling wryly, Paul nodded a greeting. His hair was a rich auburn with a touch of gray at the temples, but his eyes were the same jade green as his daughter's.

Cassie turned then to the couple who stood behind her, an attractive woman with impeccably styled golden hair and fashionably tailored clothing and a stocky, balding man with kind brown eyes and a rumpled suit. "This is my mother, Holly Bauer and my stepdad, Larry Bauer. My fiancé is running a little late. He's going to join us as soon as he can."

"I have some things to do for the wedding we're hosting this weekend. I'll leave you in my sister's capable hands," Bonnie said, backing toward the bustling dining room. "It was very nice to meet you all."

Kinley thought Bonnie avoided Paul's eyes in particular when she turned and hurried away—maybe because she was still embarrassed by the collision.

She motioned toward the conference table behind her. "Why don't you all take a seat and we'll get started. May I offer anyone something to drink? Coffee? Water?"

Making an effort to push everything but business out of her thoughts, she segued smoothly into work mode, prepared to make a dynamite presentation of the inn's wedding services to this eager bride and her family. Yet even as she gave her full attention to her potential clients, thoughts of Dan—and memories of their kisses—hovered at the back of her mind, waiting to pounce on her as soon as she let down her guard.

The Sossaman family arrived a full hour and a half earlier than necessary for the rehearsal. Obviously it was Eva's idea to be so early, since the rest of the family looked a bit harried by her nagging. Having just completed her satisfactory meeting with Cassie's family, Kinley greeted the Sossaman crew as they streamed in through the now-reopened front door of the inn.

Eva's husband, Clinton, was a stoop-shouldered accountant who'd been beaten down by life's disappointments and a relentlessly critical wife, or at least that was Kinley's private assessment of the man. Serena's brother Connor and his wife, Alicia, were the stereotypical country-club duo, owners of a successful travel agency specializing in Caribbean cruises for senior citizens. They alternated between hovering over their overly indulged son and letting him run wild, assuming another member of the family was keeping an eye on him.

As for Chris Thompson, the groom, Kinley hadn't yet figured him out. The ruddy-faced, squarely-built young man had said very little on the few occasions she'd met him, insisting that he knew nothing about "wedding stuff." Ask him about hunting, fishing or Hokies football and he'd have an opinion, he joked, but flowers and frills were out of his area of expertise. Like his mother, Chris seemed to be the make-no-waves type, nodding agreeably when his future mother-in-law spoke, rarely bothering to argue and almost always giving in quickly when he did. Kinley supposed that trait boded well for the future of his marriage.

Serena had requested a casual rehearsal followed by a low-key dinner, but Eva had dressed as if the celebrity press would be covering the event. She swept into the inn barking instructions, scrutinizing every detail of the preparations, blithely rearranging elements Bonnie had spent all day putting into place. Bonnie and Rhoda discreetly went behind her putting a few things back as they'd been, which Eva didn't even notice. She simply liked to appear to be in charge.

The midweek inn guests had mostly checked out that afternoon, to be replaced by relatives of Serena and Chris who'd come from out of town for the wedding. Eva had been annoyed when Kinley and Bonnie wouldn't relax the rule about young children for them, but Kinley had stuck to that restriction, personally making arrangements with a nearby motel to set aside a block of rooms for the wedding guests with kids. Children were welcome to attend the rehearsal dinner and the wedding, but the inn simply wasn't set up to accommodate young overnight visitors.

The weather was cooperating beautifully with the wedding plans, the temperature nicely moderate, the sky clear. This late in May, the days had grown longer, so it was still light at six o'clock, though the shadows had deepened around the edges of the garden. The sun would not yet have set when the rehearsal began at seven. It would be twilight by the time they moved in for dinner, which was scheduled to begin at eight—if

Eva didn't delay the rehearsal by making everyone walk through their parts over and over until she was satisfied.

Though she'd already reviewed the decorations, Kinley studied them again in smug satisfaction when she walked out onto the deck with the Sossaman-Thompson party. For such a grumpy pragmatist, her brother was a genius with outdoor decorations. He followed the instructions given him by wedding planners, florists or other clients, but in such a way that even they were always impressed when he finished. Somehow he'd managed to make even Eva's over-the-top requests look tasteful and elegant, skillfully weaving tulle and organza and garland and fairy lights into the landscape and around the gazebo. Bow-bedecked white iron candelabras held tall white tapers, and white plaster pedestals would hold the lush arrangements of white calla lilies, lavender roses and freesia for the wedding. The pedestals were topped now with more modest baskets of blooms that would serve as decoration for the rehearsal.

Bonnie flipped a switch and the fairy lights glowed among the lavender-and-white drapings, visible even in the daylight. The wedding party expressed the appropriate oohs and aahs in response.

White folding chairs had been arranged in rows on either side of the pebbled path from the deck to the gazebo. Knots of lavender and white tulle and white silk calla lilies had been attached at the end of each row. The officiate, groom and groomsmen would wait in the gazebo—three steps up from the ground—while the ring bearer, flower girl, bridesmaids and finally the bride and her father proceeded up the path from the deck to join them. The musicians had already set up inside the gazebo behind the altar, with a portable piano and sound equipment for the soloist. Kinley ran through her mental checklist for the umpteenth time as she let her gaze travel slowly over the scene, reassuring herself nothing had been overlooked.

Chris smiled rather shyly at Kinley and Bonnie, who stood side by side assessing their clients' reactions. "I don't know anything about wedding stuff, but this looks real nice," he said. "Doesn't it, Serena?"

The bride nodded, but Kinley still thought her smile looked strained. "It looks like a fairy tale."

"I'm glad you like it," Kinley said warmly.

Eva tapped her chin thoughtfully, her eyes narrowed in speculation. "Maybe we could just move some of the—"

"Mother!" Serena wailed. "We aren't changing another thing this late. Period."

"I can't imagine wanting to mess with perfection, anyway," Dan said, having approached the group without drawing notice. He winked quickly at Kinley before turning his full attention to Serena. "You've done a fantastic job of choosing your decorations," he assured her. "It's going to be a beautiful wedding."

Eva preened. "Yes, it will. I—I mean, Serena and I spent hours planning and discussing and looking through bridal magazines and websites for ideas. I can't tell you how much work we've put into this."

Biting the inside of her mouth, Kinley turned to welcome the groom's parents, who had just come outside to join the family admiring the landscaping. She was confirming to them that everything was on track with the caterer for the rehearsal dinner when she was interrupted by a shrill screech from Eva.

"Someone help my grandson! Save him from that beast!"

Chapter Seven

Dan was the first to react after Eva's near-hysterical scream paralyzed the group at the foot of the stairs. Moving swiftly in the direction she'd pointed with a trembling finger, he approached the boy who sat on a patch of grass just beside and slightly behind the gazebo, his face being licked by the black-and-brown dog who was growling happily while his stubby tail wagged behind him. It was quite obvious that young Grayson had absolutely no fear of the dog.

Dan slowed as he got closer, holding out a hand and speaking calmly to the dog. "Hey, there, Ninja. How's it going, buddy?"

The dog moved away from the boy to sniff Dan's hand, then lick him enthusiastically as if to demonstrate that he remembered him. His silly growl got even louder with pleasure when Dan rubbed his ears.

"Hey!" Grayson protested. "*My* dog!"

He'd barely finished speaking when his father snatched him up and hauled him away, objecting loudly, toward the perceived safety of the inn. Dan slipped two fingers under the dog's collar to hold him still, and Ninja leaned obligingly against him, making no effort to pull away.

Kinley joined them, shaking her head in dismay. "I can't believe this," she muttered.

"I'll take him back to Logan's yard," Dan offered.

"Thank you."

"Where did that creature come from?" Eva asked from a circumspect distance, which required her to raise her voice to a somewhat painfully shrill level. "Someone should call animal control immediately."

"There's no need for that, Eva. This is my brother's dog. He's completely harmless."

"Harmless? He's growling!"

"He isn't growling. That's just his way of communicating."

"He terrified my grandson. Listen to him crying."

"Mom, Grayson is crying because Connor won't let him play with the dog, not because he was afraid," Serena explained with frayed patience. "Please don't overreact."

"I'll take the dog home," Dan said again.

"I'll come with you to make sure the gate is securely fastened," Kinley volunteered immediately.

"We promise the dog will be properly restrained during the rest of the weekend," Bonnie said from behind Eva and Serena. "If you'd all like to come inside now, we're setting out appetizers in the parlor for your guests. I'm sure you'd like to visit with the wedding party as they arrive for the rehearsal."

"Come inside, Mom. Please."

Eva allowed herself to be nudged inside. Bonnie shot a quick grimace over her shoulder at Kinley and Dan, then continued to herd all the others through the back doors into the inn.

"Oh, my God," Kinley groaned, rubbing her temples with both hands. "Seriously, what next?"

Still holding the dog's collar with one hand, Dan laid his other hand on her shoulder. "Rough day, huh?"

She dropped her hands and straightened. "I've had easier. Let's get this stupid dog back to Logan's."

Unoffended, Ninja yawned, reached out his massive head, cleanly snapped off a rose blossom with his teeth and dropped it at Kinley's feet. Dan burst out laughing. Kinley was not amused.

"Let's take him back now," she said through clenched teeth as she retrieved the rose from the path and glared at the bare branch. "Before I drown the mutt in the fountain."

"Don't worry, Ninja," Dan said, urging the dog toward Logan's cottage. "She's all talk."

"I wouldn't advise him to bet his life on that," Kinley grumbled.

Grinning, Dan kept walking with the dog at his side and Kinley right behind them. The side gate into Logan's yard stood partially open when they reached it, explaining how the dog had gotten out. The signs Logan had posted were clearly evident, but had been ignored. Dan suspected it was because the perpetrator wasn't yet old enough to read.

"Grayson could definitely reach this latch," he observed, ushering Ninja inside the fence and snapping the latch into place. "It wouldn't be that hard for him to open the gate."

"You're probably right," she said, studying the gate closely. "He probably opened it last time, too. Grayson is slippery. I thought at least someone in his family was watching him this time, but obviously not."

"I think the kid needs to be on a leash more than Logan's dog does."

She laughed shortly. "You've got that right. But I'm going to tell Logan he'll have to put a lock on this gate at least until after the wedding. His signs aren't going to keep Grayson in check, and I wouldn't trust the kid's family to watch him closely enough to prevent this from happening again. It wouldn't surprise me if he managed to slip away during the wedding—and he's the ring bearer. He's supposed to stand in front of everyone the whole time."

Dan felt his brows draw down into a scowl. "People shouldn't have kids if they aren't going to take care of them," he muttered.

He felt Kinley touch his arm and he realized that once again he'd unwittingly revealed old emotions to her. What was it about her that made it so easy for him to open up to her? Oddly enough, after only a couple of days with her, he felt as though Kinley knew him better than some people he'd known for months.

She sighed lightly. "The Sossamans aren't bad parents, I guess. Just easily distracted. And they all tend to assume that everyone else is watching Grayson when it turns out that no one is."

"Pushing the kid off on everyone else, ignoring him to focus on their own personal dramas?" He felt his irritation mounting as he spoke, and he fought to bank it down. This was not the time to dwell on the past. "I just hope nothing happens to the kid while they're being 'not bad' parents."

Before she had a chance to respond, he drew a sharp breath and glanced around Logan's home. The cottage was small, but tidy, designed to fade into the background as much as possible so as not to draw attention from the inn, gazebo and gardens. "Where is your brother?"

"He had a doctor's appointment late this afternoon, after which I talked him into going out for dinner with a friend. He hasn't had a night off in weeks. He made sure everything was ready for the rehearsal before he left, and of course he'd come rushing back if I text him. But I think Ninja will stay put for now, especially if we keep an eye on Grayson."

"Yeah, I'm sure he will." Dan rattled the latch, just to be sure it was secure. "I was just curious. I usually see your brother quietly working somewhere on the grounds."

"Yeah, he's not much of a talker but he's a hard worker."

"So, what's your part in the rest of this?" he asked, nodding toward the gazebo. "Does Eva expect you to light the candles, play the piano, sing the solos and perform the ceremony?"

She laughed, but immediately smoothed her expression. "We have other people doing all those things, of course, but I'll be around in case I'm needed. I'm having to serve as de facto wedding planner in dealing with the subcontractors."

"Let me guess. Eva wanted to do all the planning, herself?"

Kinley bit her lip against another smile. "Yes."

He shook his head. "I have a feeling you'll be glad when this one is over and you can cash the check."

"I should probably get back now."

"Yes, I know. You won't talk smack about your client. I have to admire your restraint."

She cleared her throat, glanced toward the inn, then gave him a look through her lashes. "About what happened at my house earlier…"

He still felt a low thrum course through him when he thought about those kisses. About having his hands on her, having her pressed so tightly against him he'd felt the warmth of her skin through her clothes. Focused and no-nonsense Kinley Carmichael had a hotly passionate side hidden beneath those professional outfits she wore. He wondered if she even fully acknowledged that facet of her own personality.

"Thanks to that terribly timed phone call, not a lot did happen," he reminded her.

She turned to stare hard at Ninja, who had settled onto Logan's back stoop and fallen asleep, his rumbly growl changing to a gruff snore. "Probably for the best. After all, you're leaving tomorrow."

Dan moved closer to her, standing just behind her. He, too, looked at the dog, but his attention was completely focused on Kinley. "Like I said, I could hang around for a few more days. Maybe you and I could do something Sunday? You don't work Sundays, do you?"

"Actually, I do work most Sundays, either here at the inn or showing a house or just catching up on paperwork at home."

He shook his head in exasperation. There was definitely such a thing as being too focused. "But maybe you can free a couple hours this Sunday? The wedding will be over, and you'll deserve a break. Your brother isn't the only one who needs an occasional evening off, you know."

She turned her head to look at him over her shoulder. "Can you really just rearrange your schedule on a whim like that? Don't you have appointments? Schedules?"

He shrugged. "I'm flexible. I've been thinking about taking some time off. Maybe working more on my book."

"You haven't said much about the book yet. Will it be based on some of your adventures?"

He swallowed, a bit nervous as always when he talked to anyone else about the book he'd been burning to write. "I'd use some of what I learned in my travels, but the story is pure fiction. Thriller, espionage stuff— a hapless young guy caught up in something big and deadly. A friend of mine from college is a fairly well-known film producer now. We had drinks in New York one night and he said the idea intrigued him. He said he'd consider optioning the book for a film if I send it to him when it's completed."

Her face lit up with instant enthusiasm. "Wow, Dan, that's pretty great. I mean, you could write a book or a screenplay or both. Maybe turn it into a whole series. You should get an agent and maybe a publicist and a…"

"Whoa, whoa!" Laughing, he held up both hands. Her enthusiasm pleased him, but also made him even more overwhelmed about the goal he'd set for himself. What if it all came to nothing? What if he made a big deal out of the book, then struck out with it? It seemed prudent to downplay the dream, hedging his bets, in a way.

"It's still just at the early stages, an outline and a few sample chapters. My cousin wants me to keep writing for the magazine—actually, she's nagging me to take an editorial spot, but as I said before, that doesn't interest me. Maybe I'll start another series for her about interesting Southern places. Maybe I'll spotlight local legends in the next series. Like a ghostly bride who blesses couples who are lucky in love."

As he'd calculated, that comment dimmed the excitement in her expression, distracting her from his tenuous ideas for his future. "You know how I feel about that," she said flatly.

"Yes. But it's still worth consideration. I've been doing some internet research into the legend of the bride. Like you said, there's not much available. It isn't exactly a well-known tale. But there were enough reports over the years to keep it from fading completely from local memory. Certainly worth looking into."

"I can't imagine you'd rather spend your time tracking down silly old ghost stories than working on an idea that's already caught the interest of a film producer."

He'd mostly been teasing when he'd mentioned researching the ghost, but something about her tone made his defenses rise. "You sound a lot like my parents—well, you would if they approved any more of me writing a screenplay than they do of me working for my cousin. They're always reminding me that I'm not living up to my potential."

Considering what little he'd told her about his parents, he supposed he couldn't blame her for looking annoyed by the comparison. "Maybe they really do just want what's best for you," she suggested.

"That might mean something to me if I thought they

really cared about what was best for me rather than what reflected best on them."

Shaking his head, he reminded himself it was his parents who ignited his temper, not Kinley. Although there were times when she could get under his skin with that everything's-gotta-be-perfect attitude of hers, he admitted. "This isn't really the time to get into my issues. All I was asking is if you can take a little time off Sunday."

"Maybe," she said after a brief hesitation, though her shoulders were still a bit stiff. "I should probably just get through tonight and tomorrow before making any future plans."

"Think about it."

"I will." She sounded as if she wouldn't really have a choice about that. "Just one question?"

"Of course."

"Why do you want to spend more time with me when I get the distinct impression that I occasionally irritate the hell out of you?" she asked with a slightly rueful smile.

He couldn't help chuckling in response to her insight. "You do have a knack for pushing my buttons," he conceded. "In lots of ways. I can't quite explain it. I just know that from the moment I first met you, I wanted to get to know you better. That desire hasn't changed. In fact, it's only gotten stronger the more time I've spent with you."

"Yes, well, maybe we should just call it quits before I end up pushing the wrong button," she said bluntly. "It's been fun and all, but why press our luck?"

He couldn't resist reaching up to touch her soft hair, twisting a lock idly around one finger. "Still practicing risk aversion, Kinley? Hardly what I'd expect from someone so fearlessly ambitious when it comes to business."

"My number-one rule of business—play to your strengths," she reminded him. "That philosophy increases the odds of success."

"And decreases the chances of failure," he added. "The one outcome Kinley Carmichael simply won't accept."

"Maybe you are getting to know me a bit," she quipped.

He laughed softly and lowered his head to brush his lips across hers. "Not nearly as well as I'd like to."

For only a moment, her lips responded and the kiss deepened. Just enough to make him crave more. She drew back before he could do anything to satisfy that hunger. Looking quickly around, she moved away from him, smoothing her hair and straightening her clothes. It was obvious she didn't want to be seen kissing him, and he could understand that. Not only would it potentially cause gossip about what she wouldn't consider professional behavior, but there was always the specter of conflict of interest hanging over them. After all, he was here to write a review of her business.

The article had always been intended to have a positive slant, but he could see where kissing one of the owners might call into question his motives—or hers. At least in the minds of an outsider. As for himself, he'd never even considered that Kinley would stoop to flirting with him in an attempt to get a better write-up. As much as he still had to learn about her, he'd figured that out almost immediately.

"I have to get back. Eva's probably had a chance to

calm down by now. I'll assure her Ninja is safely contained."

He nodded. "He shouldn't get out again as long as he doesn't have any help."

Casting one last look at the snoozing mutt, Kinley turned and started back toward the inn. Dan followed a bit more slowly. He wasn't sure what he was going to do with himself for the next couple of days—but he knew he'd spend more time with Kinley if he got the chance. There was just something about her...

Members of the wedding party gathered on the deck, with a few out-of-town guests who were staying at the inn, for a casual cocktail hour before the rehearsal. Though it was still light out, Eva had insisted on having burning torches around the outside of the deck. Kinley lit them herself, and she had to admit they did look good. Garland with bows draped the railing, and clusters of helium-filled balloons in purple and shiny white floated above the guests.

The caterer had provided two servers for the rehearsal dinner; they mingled now with trays of champagne, lavender cosmopolitans and nonalcoholic purple grape drinks. Even the appetizers fit the lavender-and-white color scheme—sugar-frosted purple grapes with chunks of creamy white pear, cubes of soft white cheese on crisp white crackers. Soft music played from hidden speakers, low enough so as not to interfere with conversation. The photographer and videographer moved discreetly in the background, documenting the evening's activities, and nearly everyone in attendance was snapping photos with their cell phones.

As over-the-top and borderline tacky as Eva had been

at times during the months of planning, Kinley was satisfied that everything had come together well enough.
She wasn't sure there was really much of Serena's personality on display here this evening, but maybe Serena
was okay with that. Perhaps just having her parents foot
the entire bill for the wedding made it worth putting up
with her mother's bossiness.

Though Kinley and Bonnie had intended to remain
well out of sight during the wedding festivities unless they were needed, as they didn't actually know
the bridal couple other than as clients, Eva insisted
on dragging them into the party. She seemed to take
pride in introducing them as her "dear friends, the owners of Bride Mountain Inn." Because Eva fulsomely
praised their services—though usually with the subtle
caveat that they'd simply followed her directions to the
letter—Kinley allowed herself to be put on display,
though Bonnie quickly excused herself with a murmured explanation that she was needed elsewhere. Kinley figured it was good for future business. She was
drawn into a conversation with the wedding soloist
about possibly hosting a fiftieth wedding anniversary
party for her parents here, and the groom's fortysome-
thing aunt speculated that the inn would be the perfect
setting for an annual weekend retreat for some of her
sorority sisters.

Dan wasn't able to escape attention, either. Eva
caught him trying to slip upstairs and she pounced,
delighted to introduce the journalist who was there to
document her daughter's wedding for a prestigious magazine. His expression somewhat resigned, Dan didn't
even waste time trying to correct her, simply meeting
her friends with the courtesy and charm Kinley had

come to expect from him. Their gazes met at one point and he gave her a quick wink, coaxing a soft laugh from her before she turned back to the nostalgic sorority sister. As many reasons as she had to resist him, he certainly made it hard for her to remember them when he smiled at her in just that way.

She kept a discreet eye on mischievous young Grayson. So far he was being well behaved, quietly coloring with three-year-old Mallory, who would serve as flower girl, while the groom's three slightly older nephews sat cross-legged on the deck nearby engrossed in some sort of card game. Eva had made it clear in the wedding invitations that young children were not encouraged to attend the wedding festivities, so these five were the only ones present at the moment, and they were causing no trouble. Still, Kinley intended to check on Grayson periodically during the evening. Just in case.

She supposed she couldn't blame Dan—exactly—when the subject of the ghostly bride of the mountain popped up just as she was about to start herding the wedding party into place for the rehearsal. Dan was chatting with Maxine Thompson, the groom's great-aunt, listening politely as she boasted of the many charms of the Blue Ridge Highlands where she had lived for almost eighty years. "You know we're considered the true home of country music," she bragged. "And Blacksburg has been named one of the best towns in the U.S. in which to raise children. Do you have children, Mr. Phelan?"

"No, ma'am," he answered, obviously taken by the garrulous senior. "I'm not married."

She shook a crooked finger at him. "About time you

were settling down, isn't it? What are you, about thirty-five?"

"Close enough."

Sipping a lavender cosmo from a glass someone had pressed into her hand, Kinley eavesdropped shamelessly on the amusing interrogation, glad someone else was the focus of disconcerting questions for a change.

"Past time you started looking for a wife," Maxine assured him. "There are quite a few nice, single young ladies around here, some in this very wedding party. And who knows," she added with a surprisingly girlish giggle, "maybe you'll even see the ghost bride. If you do, you'll know you've found the right girl."

Kinley set down her glass and hastily and looked pointedly at her watch as she turned to Eva. "Shouldn't we—?"

"Ghost bride?" Dan asked Maxine with a disingenuous curiosity that made Kinley want to pinch him. Hard.

Maxine nodded energetically. "It's an old legend. You don't hear much about it anymore 'cause the kids don't really know it. Guess they don't have time for local folktales what with their tweeter and facepages and all that stuff."

Dan made a funny choking sound, but merely nodded encouragingly. "I've always enjoyed hearing old legends."

Kinley shot a hard look at him but he studiously avoided her gaze. She knew darned well that he was aware of her glaring at him.

"There's an old story about the bride of the mountain," Maxine began avidly while nearly everyone within hearing turned to listen. "Some say as how she found the love of her life here in ol' Virginny. They overcame a lot of obstacles to be together, but he was finally able to pop the question. She was blissfully happy as she planned a sunset wedding here on the mountainside in the spring, just about this time of year. Then, sadly, the night before her wedding, she died. The details are a little fuzzy about that—some say it was in a tragic fall, others say something burst in her head during a spirited spinning dance with her love. Apoplexy, they called it then."

"That's a terrible story, Aunt Maxine," mother-of-the-groom Nancy Thompson said with a shake of her head, her hand at her throat. "So sad."

Relishing the limelight, the older woman nodded. "Ever since, it's been said the bride visits the mountain whenever true love is present. She never got to have a life with her one true love, so she blesses those who have found theirs. It's been claimed that when a couple sees the bride, they'll share a lifetime of happiness together until death itself parts them."

"Did you ever know anyone who saw the bride?" Dan asked Maxine in fascination.

"I did." Maxine shot a rather smug look at Kinley. "Their great-niece is standing right there in front of you. Helen and Leo saw the bride the night Leo proposed here in the rose garden. Not many folks knew that. They considered it too intimate a detail to share with all but their closest friends. My late husband and Leo were quite the best of friends back in the day, and Leo let it slip one afternoon when they were out squirrel hunting. I declare, Helen could sure cook up a fine pot of squirrel and dumplings."

Having been drawn into the tale despite herself, Kinley shook off her momentary paralysis when attention turned to her. Maxine must have liberally embellished that story; there were several parts of it Kinley had never heard before. Not a surprise, really, because there were so many versions of the old legend and, as Maxine had said, not many people talked about it these days. The only real consistency was that bit about couples who saw the bride living happily ever after, the part that had so captivated Bonnie for all these years.

"Eva, we should probably start the rehearsal now," she murmured with a tap of her watch. "Dinner will be served at eight."

Eva nodded, distractedly. "Serena saw something when we were here for one of the planning meetings, didn't you, darling? Maybe it was the ghost bride you saw, blessing your union with dear Chris."

Kinley had to swallow a sigh. Of course Eva would be competitive even in this.

Serena was just as exasperated, though more openly. "I saw deer, Mom. A plain old white-tailed doe and her fawn. Jeez."

Unabashed, Eva shrugged. "Well, perhaps you'll see the bride this evening. You and Chris should keep a lookout. Now, everyone in the wedding party, let's take our places, shall we? Kinley is going to make sure everyone's in the right position and then she'll give the signal for when you're supposed to perform your parts. She'll do the same thing during the ceremony tomorrow."

"Wait, what?" Kinley blinked a few times at the mother of the bride. "I'm serving as the director?"

"Well, of course, dear. You've been organizing everything for us, after all."

"I, um—"

"I'm so sorry, Kinley. I thought she was going to ask my aunt to give the signals," Serena murmured apologetically. "We still can, if you'd prefer us to do so."

"No, this is fine." Sighing inwardly, Kinley rushed to organize everyone. "You and your bridesmaids go into the inn with your dad and the ring bearer and flower girl," she instructed Serena, briskly taking charge. "You'll be making your appearance from there. I'll, um, text Bonnie when to start sending you out," she said, hastily improvising.

After making a quick, confirming call to her sister, she turned to the groom and his groomsmen, the officiate and musicians, making shooing motions with her hands to get them into position. She was aware that Dan was standing off to one side, watching her improvisations with a broad grin, but she didn't have time to deal with him just then. She would definitely talk with him later, she vowed.

"Oh, my God." Kinley laid her aching head on the table in Bonnie's apartment an hour and ten minutes later, groaning heartily. The wedding party was gathered upstairs in the dining room, in the capable hands of the caterer and her staff now—at least for the next hour or so. Still, Kinley wouldn't be at all surprised to be texted by Eva at least once during the rehearsal dinner. Eva wasn't particularly happy that she and her husband weren't the official hosts of that meal, and she would surely do something during the evening to draw attention to herself.

Bonnie had made a pot of vegetable soup and a pan of corn bread for herself and Kinley and Dan, whom she'd invited to join them again. Normally Kinley wouldn't have allowed herself to show weakness in front of their guest, but the past hour had seriously tried her patience.

Bonnie set a steaming bowl in front of Kinley. "Eat. You'll feel better."

Straightening in her chair, she drew a deep breath. "Only if it's laced with vodka."

Laughing softly, Bonnie dropped into her own seat and picked up her spoon. "You don't mean that."

"No," Kinley admitted. "But if anyone could drive me to drink, it would be Eva Sossaman."

"You shouldn't talk about your 'best friend forever' that way," Dan murmured, spreading butter on a bite of corn bread.

Kinley turned to point her spoon at him accusingly. "And you. Encouraging Maxine to tell that absurd ghost story."

"I didn't bring it up, she did," he reminded her before popping the corn bread into his mouth.

"You egged her on."

He shrugged. "She wanted to tell the story, I wanted to hear it. I found it fascinating, as did most of the other people who were listening, apparently."

"Dan told me what Maxine said," Bonnie observed. "It was very sad. I hadn't heard it quite that way before."

"She was probably embroidering the tale a bit," Kinley said, voicing her earlier suspicion. "I hope you aren't planning to print a story an old woman possibly made up on the spot," she added to Dan.

"I could credit it to a longtime local," he said off-handedly. "I probably won't go into that much detail, but I would be remiss not to mention the old legend at least in passing. People go for that sort of thing these days, you know. I'm surprised you aren't jumping on a possible marketing angle—and yes, I know you said you were afraid it would attract the wrong kind of attention, but business is business, right?"

"The sweet, romantic story our great-uncle shared with our family was very special to us," Bonnie interceded. "It always affected him very deeply to talk about it. I think Kinley is reluctant to commercialize the legend, to exploit it as a cheap marketing gimmick."

"Actually, I'm looking at it from a practical business angle. Just as a ghost legend would attract some guests, it would turn others away," Kinley said brusquely. "Not to mention that we'd get tired of answering questions about it, or assuring people that they're seeing fog or deer or shadows and not ghosts. Or comforting brides who'd be disappointed by not seeing the ghost."

She looked at Dan again. "You heard Eva out there, trying to convince Serena she's already seen the bride. Before the weekend is over, Eva's probably going to demand that I produce the ghost as a part of the package she's paid for."

"Want me to dress up in a sheet?" Bonnie asked. Dan laughed, but Kinley only glared at her sister.

"I won't exploit your family legend," Dan promised. "I won't even mention that your great-aunt and great-uncle saw the bride. I'll simply make a passing reference to a charming old local legend once connected to the inn. My article wouldn't be complete without it."

"You have to give him that, Kinley. I'm sure Dan will be very tasteful in his write-up."

Kinley sighed. "Fine."

"You know why you're really so resistant to this legend?" Dan asked conversationally.

She frowned. "I've already explained that."

"I think you're a little afraid of it."

She huffed in disbelief at his suggestion. "I'm so not afraid of ghosts."

"You're afraid of things you can't control," he corrected. "You can't control ghosts—or whether or not people claim to see them on your property. And that bugs the hell out of you."

"You know what, Kinley? I think he's got you figured out," Bonnie said, sounding impressed. "I've always wondered why the ghost bride made you so uncomfortable. Maybe it's because you can't get her to appear on schedule, can't add her to your annotated and color-coded calendar."

Scowling, Kinley shifted in her chair and crumbled corn bread between her fingers. "You're both nuts."

Before they could argue any more her phone vibrated in her pocket. She drew it out and checked the screen, then sighed and stood. "Eva wants to ask my opinion about something for tomorrow."

"She's probably decided she wants a Cinderella coach and six white horses to carry Serena down the aisle." Bonnie shook her head in disapproval. "You've only eaten half your soup."

"I'm not very hungry, anyway. You two go ahead and finish your dinners. I'll see you later."

She wasn't particularly displeased that Eva had summoned her, she thought as she left the apartment and headed up the stairs. For once, the woman's timing had been just right.

Bonnie propped her elbows on the table and laced her fingers together, studying Dan across the table. "You really seem to enjoy playing with fire."

Swallowing another spoonful of the excellent soup, he chuckled. "On occasion, perhaps."

Especially when that fire was packaged within the enigma that made up Kinley Carmichael, he added silently.

"You're liable to get burned, you know. Kinley doesn't like being embarrassed."

He lifted an eyebrow. "You think I embarrassed her?"

"Well, you certainly put her at a loss for words. That doesn't happen often with Kinley."

"I didn't mean to either embarrass her or render her speechless," Dan said candidly. "I was just making an observation. And maybe teasing her a little."

"I wasn't criticizing. I think it's good for her to be shaken up a little on occasion. You're right, you know. Kinley tries too hard to stay in control. She's done it since she was a kid, but especially since her marriage broke up. Um, you did know she was married once?"

"Yes, she told me."

"Oh. Interesting. She doesn't like to talk about it."

"We didn't get into an in-depth discussion of it or anything, but she told me she married young, that it didn't last long and that her ex-husband decided he didn't want to be married."

Bonnie nodded, her expression solemn. "I wouldn't say he broke her heart, exactly, but he hurt her."

"I got that. Shook her confidence."

"Yes. And she's been determined ever since that no one will put her in that position again. It didn't help that our brother suffered a couple of painful betrayals— one by a woman he loved, another by a man he thought was a friend. I guess you could say they both have some trust issues as a result of all those betrayals. Logan dealt with it by becoming a bit of a hermit, limiting his social interactions, such as they are, to us and a very select few others."

"And Kinley dealt with it by staying in control. Always."

Bonnie inclined her head in a silent confirmation.

He was a little puzzled by this conversation. "Why are you telling me this? Something tells me you don't discuss your siblings' personal business very often."

"I don't," she agreed. "And that's all I'm saying tonight. I just thought there were a couple things you should know if you want to get closer to Kinley. And I've gotten the distinct impression that you do want that."

Did her confidences indicate her approval? "I do want to get closer to her. I mean, I know I've only just met her, but…well, there it is."

"Something clicked."

"Yeah." He supposed that described it as well as anything. "Something clicked."

Bonnie's faint sigh sounded just a bit envious. He didn't suspect for a minute that she wanted his attention for herself. He liked Bonnie a lot, but had felt no romantic chemistry with her—and he was quite certain she felt the same way about him. But maybe she was hoping to experience that click for herself with someone.

As for him—he hadn't been looking. Hadn't been prepared. Wasn't sure exactly how to proceed now that it had happened to him. He only knew that he would be staying around to see where this led. And it didn't hurt to have Kinley's sister on his side.

Chapter Eight

Eva and her family were the last nonresidential attendees to leave the rehearsal dinner. Most of the out-of-town guests who were staying at the inn had retired early to their suites, while a few others lingered in the parlor. The catering staff efficiently cleared away all evidence of the dinner. Bonnie, Rhoda and Kinley waited to set up for breakfast; it wouldn't take them long. Kinley hoped to be home by ten. Tomorrow would start early, and she wasn't sure how well she was going to sleep that night, anyway. She had a sneaky suspicion she'd have some trouble clearing her mind for sleep—and exactly who she'd be thinking of as she tossed and turned in her bed.

"We should all go, too," Serena announced after her in-laws departed. "I'm getting tired and I'll look like a hag tomorrow if I don't get some rest."

"I'll take you home whenever you're ready, honey,"

her fiancé offered immediately. "Then I'm meeting the guys for drinks—my low-key bachelor party," he added with a good-natured laugh.

Serena nodded. Kinley privately believed Serena could use a few drinks that evening, herself—or at least a couple hours away from her mother just to relax and have fun with friends, but she hadn't heard about any such plans, and it certainly wasn't her place to suggest it.

"I'm ready," Serena said. "Kinley and Bonnie have things to do here. Mom? You coming?"

Eva looked around the room again, as if trying and failing to come up with one final detail to oversee before letting go of today, then nodded and tucked her pocketbook beneath her arm. "Fine. Let's go. You should get to bed early tonight, Serena, so you'll look fresh and radiant tomorrow. I'll make you a cup of herbal tea when we get home and perhaps we'll do a facial before you turn in."

"Fine. Whatever."

Kinley noted that the once-acquiescent and unruffled Serena was becoming more tense and peevish as the hours passed toward her wedding. Bridal jitters were quite common, of course, but she was a little concerned about Serena. The bride looked to be one mother-nag away from a total meltdown. If they could only get through the next twenty-four hours, Serena would move into her own home with her husband—and at twenty-five, it was past time for her to move out of her parents' home, in Kinley's opinion. Perhaps it would have been even better if Serena had lived on her own for a year or two, but then maybe Kinley was just projecting her own experience onto the younger woman.

"Where are Connor and Alicia and Grayson?" Eva asked.

"They're in the parlor, I think, talking with the Barringtons," Chris replied. "I saw them in there earlier."

Serena turned toward the doorway. "I'll let them know we're leaving."

"I've told everyone in the wedding party to be dressed and ready at least an hour before the ceremony begins at five tomorrow," Eva said to Kinley—unnecessarily since Kinley had heard Eva barking orders earlier. "Oh, Bonnie, there you are. I wanted to make sure there will be fresh coffee available all day tomorrow. Many of our guests will arrive early and will probably enjoy sipping coffee and mingling in here until time to be seated for the ceremony."

Kinley looked around to see that Bonnie and Dan had wandered in behind her. Her eyes met Dan's, and she thought he studied her rather intently for a moment before he smiled. Just what had he and Bonnie talked about after she'd left them?

"I'll have coffee, pitchers of ice water and fresh fruit available in here all day tomorrow," Bonnie promised Eva patiently.

"Good. Now, Kinley—"

Serena reentered the room and interrupted whatever additional command Eva had intended to issue. "Dad, Alicia said she left Grayson with you."

Clinton raised his eyebrows above the rims of his narrow glasses. "He was with me earlier, but he got whiny so I sent him to find his mom in the parlor. I reminded him there were games in there and he said he wanted to go play."

"He's not in there."

Connor and Alicia entered the dining room, both looking around. "Grayson's with you, isn't he, Dad? You were showing him the bird's nest in that bush around front."

"I sent him inside. I saw him walk through the front door with my own eyes," Clinton insisted. "I stayed outside to exchange a few words with Mike Ray before he left, but I know Grayson came in."

"Okay, so he's probably somewhere here in the inn," Connor said with an edge of anxiety to his voice. "Let's all split up and look for him. Maybe he's gone upstairs with someone in the family who thinks he had permission to go with them."

"We'll spread out and look," Bonnie said instantly. "Connor and Alicia, Chris and Serena, run upstairs and start knocking on doors. The rest of us will look on this floor. Feel free to look anywhere—even the attic. Maybe he's exploring."

Kinley and Dan shared a somber look and she sensed that he had the same thought she did.

"Dan and I are going to look outside," she said quickly. She held up the phone in her hand. "Everyone has Eva's number, right? So call her if you find him, and she'll call me."

Already fussing loudly about how she couldn't depend on anyone to do anything, even watch out for her grandson, Eva dug her phone out of her purse as Kinley and Dan hurried out of the room. She led him into the kitchen, seeing no signs of the boy there or on the way, grabbed a couple of flashlights from a kitchen drawer and shoved one at Dan. The sun had set during dinner, and while the grounds were well lit, there were still a few dark nooks in which the boy could hide, if he wanted.

Without need for discussion, they headed straight for Logan's cottage. If Grayson had slipped outside unnoticed, there was a good chance he'd made a beeline for Ninja. Even from the gazebo, Kinley could see that Logan's truck wasn't parked in his drive, so he hadn't yet returned home from his rare evening out.

"I can't believe no one watches that kid," Dan said angrily.

"There was a lot of confusion with the wedding rehearsal and all the guests the family hadn't seen in a long—" Hearing herself making excuses, Kinley stopped with a frown. "You're right, of course. They should have watched him more closely, especially since they all know Grayson is prone to wandering off."

"The least they could do is hire a nanny if they don't want to take care of him, themselves. My parents at least kept a nanny around at all times."

Hearing the old resentment simmering in his taut voice, Kinley wondered if Dan identified in some ways with young Grayson. It made her sad to think of Dan as a lonely, neglected little boy. Grayson wasn't always watched closely, but at least his family was very affectionate with him most of the time.

Her heart sank when Ninja came running to the other side of the gate in Logan's yard, with no sign of the boy in sight. "He's not here."

Dan made a slow, complete turn, carefully scanning the deepening shadows as far as he could see from that point. "No."

Kinley's phone vibrated in her hand and she let out a little sigh of relief. "Maybe they've found him. Hello?"

"We can't find him anywhere in the inn." Bonnie sounded genuinely alarmed. "People are still looking in every closet and cranny where he could be hiding, but nothing so far. Everyone in the inn is joining the hunt. We're going to start searching the grounds now."

Shaking her head in answer to Dan's unspoken question, Kinley closed her eyes and pinched the bridge of her nose, trying to think where the boy could have gone. She pictured the hiking trail entrance at the back of the property, framed by cascading wisteria and marked with a sign the boy was too young to read. There was a side path to the trail from Logan's cottage. The trail wasn't lit; surely the boy wouldn't have gone off in the woods in the dark? "Maybe you should call Logan. Should we contact the authorities?"

"One of the wedding guests staying with us is a retired sheriff's deputy. He said we should make a thorough search of the inn and the immediate grounds first and then call."

"Okay. Dan and I are going to carry the search farther out. We'll start down the trail, beginning at Logan's. Have someone look from the trailhead there in the garden. Stay in touch."

As she disconnected the call and started to direct Dan toward the path, she heard a rattle from the gate. She and Dan both looked around in time to see the dog push hard against the gate latch with his nose and one paw. Before either of them could react, the gate was open and the dog shot past them, his black-and-brown body disappearing into the darkening woods.

"Crap!" Kinley dashed after the dog, silently cursing herself for wearing a dress today. Underbrush scratched her bare legs as she plunged into the woods on the narrow path, but at least she'd had the sense to wear comfortable shoes when she'd left her house that morning. "Ninja! Grayson!" she called out.

Staying right behind her, Dan released an ear-piercingly sharp whistle. "Ninja!" he shouted.

Kinley turned on her flashlight. Beneath the canopy of trees, it was hard to see more than a couple of feet ahead. She didn't want to think of young Grayson possibly wandering around the woods in the darkness. He could fall in a hole or off a ledge, encounter less-than-friendly wildlife, or tumble into the spring-swollen creek that ran down the hillside not far from the inn. "Grayson! Ninja!"

Her phone buzzed again, raising her hopes, but it was only Bonnie reporting that there was still no sign. Search teams had been sent down the road toward the café, and were organizing into grids to cover as much ground as possible. The authorities had been contacted, and a search-and-rescue team was being dispatched.

"We'll keep looking out here," Kinley said grimly. She called the boy's name again after disconnecting, taking only a moment to listen fruitlessly for an answer before pushing on.

A sharp stick scraped her right calf and she gasped in pain. Dan caught her arm. "Are you okay?"

"I'm wishing I'd worn pants." She pushed her hair from her face with the hand holding her phone, aiming her flashlight ahead with the other.

Dan pointed his light down at her leg. "You're bleeding."

"It's a scratch. I'm really worried about Grayson, Dan. If he wandered off the trail, he could be in trouble. There are several places he could fall, and there's a creek that's deeper than usual because of all that rain we had earlier this month. It runs downhill, pretty swift in spots."

He squeezed her shoulder. "We'll find him."

"Do you think Ninja is looking for him? Or is with him now?"

"I think that's a good guess. He sure seemed to have a goal when he lit out of there."

Kinley turned to shout into the woods. "Ninja! Grayson!"

She held her breath as she listened for a response, sensed Dan doing the same. All they heard were other voices calling out the boy's name from the direction of the inn and the hiking trail.

"Does the dog ever bark?" Dan asked, moving with her when she started walking again, hoping she was still going in the direction the dog had run.

"If he does, I've never heard him. Only that funny sound he makes. Grayson!"

"At least we know how he's been getting out of the fence. The dog is smarter than you've all given him credit for."

"I hope so," she said sincerely, praying Ninja was taking care of the child even now.

As comfortable as they were, her shoes were not made for tramping through the woods. She stepped carefully as she regularly called out the boy's and the dog's names, but when a loose stone rolled beneath the smooth sole of one of her shoes, she went down hard. A choked cry escaped her when pain shot through her, but she gritted her teeth and struggled to her feet with Dan's help.

"Are you hurt?" he asked urgently, holding her forearms.

She pushed the pain aside. "No. We're getting close to the creek, Dan. If he fell in…"

He slipped an arm around her shoulders to give her a bracing hug. "We'll find him, Kinley."

She leaned against him for one weak-kneed moment, both of them looking around the now-dark woods, trying to decide which way one curious little boy might have gone. They weren't on the hiking trail, though they could hear voices calling from that direction, so there was no clear path for them to follow. The ground beneath the trees was covered with leaves and needles and clusters of spiky brush. Kinley and her siblings had played in these woods as children and she knew how easy it was to get lost in them. She and Dan were plunging blindly through the trees, with no clear direction, no plan of action. And even worse, fog was beginning to roll in, wispy tendrils winding through the trees and hovering over the ground. What if…?

Something moved at the corner of her field of vision to her left, and she turned quickly in that direction. Dan turned, too, so he must have seen it, as well. They both aimed their flashlights in that direction, sweeping the hillside with the narrow beams. Dan's beam stopped abruptly, then rapidly backtracked. Kinley followed the direction of the light, then gasped. She would have sworn she saw a feminine form almost hidden by the trees, beckoning to them. For just a moment, she saw a face in that ring of light. A woman's face. Smiling at them.

The light jerked in Dan's hand. By the time he steadied it, the…whatever it had been was gone. A thin line of fog snaked around the undergrowth in that area, but beyond that was nothing but darkness.

Kinley looked up at Dan with widened eyes, telling herself that pain and panic must be causing her to see things that weren't there. He couldn't possibly have seen what she did, right?

His face looked a little pale in the periphery of the flashlight beam, his expression quite grim. Because of his worry about Grayson…or because he, too, had seen something he couldn't quite explain?

By unspoken agreement, they moved in unison toward the area where she thought she'd seen someone.

"Call them again, Dan," she gasped, stumbling over a stick but righting herself without his assistance. "My voice is giving out."

He cupped his hands around his mouth and gave another shrill whistle, followed by the boy's name and the dog's.

Kinley started to move forward again. Dan stopped her. "Wait."

She opened her mouth to question him, but he shushed her quickly, then whistled again, the sound spearing through the heavy shadows. "Ninja? *Grayson!*"

She heard it, too, this time. A faint, rusty-sounding bark from somewhere north and downhill from them. "Ninja?" she called eagerly.

Stumbling and sliding, they followed the occasional bark, flashlight beams waving wildly as they moved with as much haste as safely possible. Kinley heard the slap of a branch, heard Dan mutter a pained curse, but she was afraid to slow down and check on him. It didn't sound as though Ninja was moving, but she was concerned about finding him. She didn't even want to think that Grayson wouldn't be with the dog. She and Dan were putting a lot of faith in Ninja's tracking abilities, considering they really had no idea if he'd run after the missing child or a stray cat. Her phone was being stubbornly silent, indicating that the boy had not yet been found, so she and Dan had to follow this lead, no matter how tenuous.

She skidded to a stop with a choked sob when her light fell on a pale little face and a pair of glittering canine eyes.

Dirty and disheveled, Grayson sat on the ground, his arms around Ninja, who sat beside him now making his usual rumble-sound. Grayson wasn't crying, perhaps because the dog had given him courage, but his lip quivered when he looked up at Kinley and Dan.

"I saw a deer," he said. "And then I got lost."

Every muscle in Kinley's body seemed to sag suddenly in relief. The pain she'd been trying to ignore flooded through her, but she tamped it down again.

"Call it in," Dan advised her, then moved past her to kneel in front of the boy. "Hey, sport. Ready to go see your mom and dad?"

"Can the doggie come?"

"Sure, he can come with us. Let's go, Ninja."

Straightening, he scooped the boy into his arms, cradling him close in visible relief. The dog wagged its stubby tail and grinned up at them.

Kinley put in a quick call to Bonnie, figuring it would be best to let her sister break the good news to the family in person. Reassured that the child was safe and unharmed, Bonnie let out a gasp of joy, then promised to start calling in all the search teams.

"So," Dan was saying to Grayson. "A deer, huh?"

His arms looped comfortably around Dan's neck, the boy nodded. "A big deer. It had horns."

"Yeah? Well, next time you'd better tell someone before you chase after anything, okay? Your family was really worried about you." Dan looked at Kinley. "This way, right?" he asked, nodding toward his left.

Roused from the overwhelmed immobility that had briefly gripped her, she swallowed, nodded and limped in the direction of the inn. Though she concentrated fiercely on the light ahead, and on carefully placing her feet so she didn't stumble, she couldn't help but look rather nervously out of the corners of her eyes at every curl of mist, every breeze-rustled branch. To her relief, she saw no more faces in the fog, which only proved in her mind that she'd simply let her fear for Grayson play tricks on her imagination.

What else could it have been?

Kinley hobbled into her house less than an hour after returning Grayson to his frantic family. They seemed to realize how very fortunate they were with the outcome of this particular incident that could all too easily have ended in tragedy. She hoped that in the future the family would be more vigilant with the child.

Bonnie had wanted her to stay and let her tend to the scrapes and scratches Kinley had sustained in the search, but she'd begged off, saying she just wanted to go home and take a hot shower. She had slipped away during the chaos after the boy's return, not wanting to stay and rehash the search. She was still badly shaken—only by the awareness of what could have happened, she assured herself. Not by anything she'd imagined she saw during the hunt.

She turned on her bedroom light, then winced when she spotted her reflection in the cheval mirror standing in the corner. Her hair was a mess. A smudge of dirt streaked her cheek, probably from where she'd wiped her face after picking herself up from her fall. Her formerly spotless coral dress was dirty and badly wrinkled. Dried blood smeared her right leg from the deep scrape that ran diagonally beneath her knee toward her ankle. Her knees were filthy from her fall, and a dark bruise was forming on her right shin.

None of the injuries were serious, but she would most definitely be sore tomorrow—and she didn't even want to think about what her legs would look like once all these bruises bloomed. She'd planned to wear a pretty spring dress for the wedding, but now she thought she'd choose a nice pants set, instead. And perhaps she would suggest the best man keep Grayson on a leash during the ceremony.

The thought of a long, hot bath crossed her mind, but she was too tired to wait for the tub to fill. Instead, she took a quick shower, lathering carefully around the cuts, scrubbing her face and hair while trying not to think about anything that had happened during the past twenty-four hours. She suspected her dreams would be haunted by visions of glittering blue eyes, roguish smiles, missing children and unnerving amorphous shapes in the trees. No need to dwell on any of those images any sooner than necessary.

She wrapped a soft green terry robe around her and towel-dried her hair, wondering if she had enough energy in reserve to make a cup of tea. She was still too wired to sleep, but she didn't want to obsess about... things, either. Maybe she'd just slip into some comfy pj's, turn on the TV and watch something fluffy and mindless.

Her doorbell rang just as she opened a drawer to pull out a cami and sleep shorts. She bit her lip. She wasn't expecting anyone, but somehow she knew who was at her doorstep. After only a moment, she sighed and tightened the front of her robe.

Like her, Dan must have taken a quick shower. His thick, dark hair was still just a little damp around his face. An angry red scratch striped his right cheek, alarmingly close to his eye. He wore a clean gray T-shirt and a pair of faded jeans, which he'd obviously thrown on quickly with a pair of sneakers. He'd been in a hurry. His gaze swept her quickly and she was suddenly, keenly aware that she wore nothing but a thin terry robe.

His bright blue eyes rose, held hers captive. "Do you want me to leave?"

She knew she should send him away. Knew what a mistake it would be to invite him in, especially tonight when her emotions were so raw, so close to the surface. Her legs ached, her raw palms stung, she was already feeling the throb of sore muscles...and yet, all she wanted to do was drag him inside and wrap herself around him.

Still looking at her, he took a step backward as she remained silent, obviously prepared to go. She felt her heart jump into her throat, and she spoke huskily around it, her voice little more than a whisper. "Stay."

Two steps forward and he was inside, the door closing solidly behind him. One step more and she was in his arms, his mouth on hers, her arms around his neck. His tongue plunged hungrily into her mouth, fusing them together, stoking the heat inside her until she felt as though she would spontaneously combust against him. Every time they kissed her reactions to him grew stronger, more urgent. Maybe she could find the strength somehow to call a stop now, before this went any further—but she wasn't sure she wanted to. Who knew when she would feel this way again, if ever?

His hand slipped between them, easing into the wrapped front of her robe, fingertips just brushing the swell of her breast. She moaned softly into his mouth, letting the last of her resistance slip away. A shift of her weight, and her breast was in his hand, his thumb slowly rubbing, circling, sending her pulse rate sky-rocketing, her thoughts whirling.

Her robe fell open. His T-shirt was soft against her breasts, his jeans rough against her thighs. She could feel his heat through the fabric, feel his arousal pressing urgently against her abdomen. Her fingers clenched in his hair, holding his mouth against hers as their tongues tangled, sparred, caressed. He cupped her bottom in his hands and hauled her even closer, so that not a breath separated them.

His clothes were an annoyance now. She tugged impatiently at the neckline of his shirt, aching to feel him against her. Dan drew back from her just far enough to grab the hem of his shirt and sweep it over his head. Even as he tossed it aside, her hands and lips were on him, gliding over ridges and planes, tracing, touching, tasting. Savoring.

The rumble that sounded from deep in his chest reminded her for a moment of Ninja. She smiled against his flat, brown nipple, but her momentary amusement evaporated when he took her mouth again.

She was distantly aware of the aches and bruises when she led him to her bed. When she fell with him into the pillows. When she rolled with him on the soft sheets. The discomfort was immaterial, overpowered by the haze of passion he stoked in her with his skilled hands and lips. He was excruciatingly thorough in his exploration, lingering and delaying until they were both on the edge of madness.

He dug in the pocket of his discarded jeans just as she was about to reach for the drawer of her nightstand. Protection dealt with, they concentrated again on pleasure.

It was no surprise to her that Dan was a patient and generous lover. She was, however, astonished by the uninhibitedly passionate side of herself he uncovered. Some time after the echoes of their choked gasps and groans had faded into deep, slowly steadying breathing, she was still dazed by the raw power of the emotions that had exploded inside her.

Eventually, of course, the haze had to clear. Her besotted smile began to fade as doubt and misgiving crept back into her mind.

Reclining on one elbow beside her, Dan reached out to touch the light crease between her eyebrows. "And she's back," he murmured.

She tried to smile, but she wasn't sure how successful she was with it.

He ran his thumb across her lower lip. He still smiled, but his eyes were serious when he asked, "Regrets?"

"No. No," she repeated more firmly. "I'm just... tired."

Scared, a tiny voice whispered inside her, but she ignored it.

She reached up to trace the scratch on his cheek with the tip of her forefinger. Though it wasn't deep, it was a bit puckered, the edges slightly reddened. "That looks as though it would sting."

"A bit. Not much."

"You're lucky it didn't get in your eye."

"Yeah. Just wasn't paying attention to the branches around me." He pushed himself upright on the bed, looking over her own scrapes and contusions. "You're okay? I'm afraid I wasn't very gentle earlier."

She smiled faintly. "I didn't want gentleness then."

He stretched out beside her again and gathered her into his arms. "Would you take it now?"

She rested her cheek on his shoulder and sighed as he pulled the sheet over them. "Yes. For a while."

For some reason she'd felt the need to remind him— remind them both—that this was only temporary. That she neither expected nor wanted anything more than this, a few hours of escape with him.

She let her thoughts drift, allowed herself to focus only on the feel of his skin beneath her cheek, the warmth of him surrounding her, the rough length of his leg tangled with her smooth one. She wasn't asleep but she was in a light doze when Dan spoke again, sounding almost tentative.

"Kinley?"

"Mmm?"

"Are we ever going to talk about it?"

That brought her eyes open, her frown back. "Talk about what?" she asked gruffly, though she was afraid she knew.

"What we saw."

She kept her head burrowed into his shoulder, her face hidden from his gaze. "We didn't see anything. A trick of the fog. That's all."

"And yet you knew exactly what I was referring to." There was a grim satisfaction in his voice, as though she had inadvertently confirmed something he'd questioned.

"I saw shadows so deep our flashlights hardly penetrated them. I saw branches swaying in the breeze and tendrils of fog winding through the woods. I saw a few stars when I fell and hit my knee on a rock. And then I heard Ninja barking and saw that Grayson was safe, and that was the only thing that really mattered."

He'd listened without reaction to her fervent assertion. She recited the words as if she'd memorized them—because she had. She'd silently repeated the spiel to herself all evening, ever since they'd left those dark woods. She had almost convinced herself it was the complete story of her experience tonight.

"Okay, fine," he said after a moment, his tone gentle, perhaps in response to the sharp edge even she had heard in her own voice. "Rest tonight. We'll talk tomorrow."

"Not about that."

He hesitated long enough for her to know that he wanted to argue. He released his breath in a hard sigh. "You really can be stubborn."

She didn't answer. He certainly wasn't the first to point it out.

"I should go, I guess."

Her fingers tightened reflexively on his arm. For some reason, she really didn't want to be alone just then. Maybe because she wanted to make the most of every minute she had with Dan before he finished his assignment and moved on.

"Stay awhile," she murmured, looking up at him through her lashes. "If you want."

He hesitated a moment, then lifted her chin with the edge of his hand. She could almost see the momentary impatience fade from his eyes as his gaze locked with hers.

"I want," he assured her and pressed his mouth to hers.

Reaching up to him, she sank into the kiss, clearing her mind again of anything but the satisfaction of being with him at that moment.

Chapter Nine

The weather Saturday was as perfect as the TV pundits had promised, with temperatures in the low seventies and blue skies dotted with only a few puffy white clouds. Having awakened alone in her bed, Kinley took another long shower, letting the hot water pulse against muscles that weren't all sore from the tramp through the woods. Just the memory of the enthusiastically energetic lovemaking that had followed made her shiver despite the warmth of the water.

After one quick assessment in the mirror, she shook her head and dived into the closet to find clothes to hide the bruises. She settled on loose buff-colored pants with a thin, very pale yellow blazer and a matching lace-trimmed camisole. Pushing the jacket sleeves up on her forearms, she added a couple of bangle bracelets and earrings. She had applied her makeup carefully and brushed her hair to the usual sleek, shiny bob. Fi-

nally satisfied that she looked put together and professional, dressed appropriately for an afternoon spring
wedding, she hooked the strap of her leather tote bag
over her shoulder and headed to her car.

She wasn't quite sure when Dan had slipped out last
night. She'd roused only long enough to lock up behind
him, as he'd insisted, and had then collapsed back into
the bed without looking at the clock. She figured it
would be a little awkward seeing him again today, but
she could handle it. They were both adults, both experi-
enced, had gone into this with eyes open and emotions
guarded. It had been quite a week, and maybe it would
take her a few days to recover—but that didn't mean
she had let herself fall for Dan. Not seriously, anyway.
Or, if she had, she'd get over it. Eventually.

Truth be told, she was more nervous about his insistence on discussing what they'd seen—what they
thought they'd seen, she corrected herself immediately—in the woods last night. Though she was confident that she'd explained that momentary aberration to
her own satisfaction since, she still couldn't help casting
a quick, sideways glance toward the woods when she
parked in her usual spot behind the inn, next to Bonnie's
car. Fortunately, all she saw on the grounds was a hive
of activity getting ready for the wedding later that day.

She'd deliberately come in a bit later than usual, after
breakfast service. She hadn't been needed for that, and
she had a busy day ahead as it was, especially since
Eva had drafted her as the last-minute wedding director. She headed straight for the coffeemaker when she
went inside, filled a cup, took a bracing sip and only
then greeted her sister and the various others milling
around the dining room.

"Logan put a lock on the gate last night," Bonnie told her when they had a chance to speak in private in the kitchen. "Now that we know Ninja is capable of opening the latch himself, we didn't want to risk him crashing the wedding later."

"I'm glad to hear that," Kinley said in relief. "I was going to insist on a lock, anyway. I'm happy Logan took care of it already."

"Have you had anything to eat this morning?"

Taking another swig of strong coffee, she shook her head. "I'm not really hungry."

Bonnie frowned. "You should eat something. You have a long day ahead."

"I'll eat later. How did breakfast go?"

"No problems. Rhoda got here early to help. She and Sandy will clean the rooms while everyone is busy with wedding festivities. Everything else seems to be on track."

Kinley had her phone in her hand, scrolling through her checklist for the day. "Eva's already called me twice with nitpicky instructions, but she's staying busy most of the day supervising Serena and all the bridesmaids at the salon. They're all getting mani-pedis and facials and having their hair and makeup done, and I wouldn't be surprised if Eva has to approve each one individually."

She'd spoken quietly but still Bonnie glanced quickly toward the doorway even as she smiled. "You're probably right," she murmured. "I just hope someone's keeping a close eye on Grayson today. You'd think he'd have been frightened enough to learn a lesson last night, but he didn't seem perturbed. Maybe his parents were scared enough to learn their lesson, instead."

"He said he was chasing a deer." Kinley shook her

head grimly. "That kid would give me a heart attack before he turns five if I were responsible for him."

"I heard him telling his parents about the deer as they were leaving, when you were getting your bag and keys. He said it was a big deer with horns, but it ran away and he got lost. He said he waited with the doggie and the nice lady and he wasn't scared."

"He wouldn't have thought I was so nice if I'd chewed him out the way I really wanted to," Kinley muttered.

"That's the odd thing," Bonnie mused, studying Kinley with a slight frown. "When Connor asked Grayson if he was talking about you, Grayson said, no, the other lady. He started talking about Ninja again then, and they took him home, but I wasn't sure what he meant. Do you know?"

Her hand suddenly unsteady, Kinley set her coffee mug carefully by the sink. "I don't even try to understand Grayson. I should probably go make some calls now, unless you need me for anything."

"No, everything's under control. Um—unless you want to talk to me? About anything?"

Kinley didn't quite meet her sister's eyes. "I don't know what you mean."

Bonnie sighed loudly. "You really think I don't know when something is going on with you? Something that's troubling you? Do you want to tell me about it?"

What, exactly, would she tell Bonnie if she tried to share what was on her mind? About the incredible night she'd spent in her bed with the footloose writer she had known less than a week? About her hollow suspicion that her feelings for him had grown too serious despite her best efforts to keep it casual? Her fear that it would be much harder than she hoped to get over him? That she would spend a very long time remembering him, wondering about him, wishing she could experience those amazing hours with him again?

Or…she swallowed hard…should she whisper to her sister that she'd seen something in the woods she couldn't explain? Something that even now she was reluctant to examine too closely in her memories, something that discomfited her even though she was 99 percent certain she and Dan had simply allowed fear, disorientation and fog to get tangled up with an improbable old tale. Sure, it was odd that they'd thought they saw the same thing at the same time—but wasn't that how old tales got started and perpetrated? The fog did look alive at times, moving and drifting and changing shapes. As simple as that.

It was just that nothing else about her feelings for Dan was simple, or easily waved off as illusion. And she didn't know how to process that reality herself, much less discuss it with her sister. Especially now, she reminded herself with another glance at her phone screen, with so much to do today.

"I'd better call the florist," she said. "She should be at the shop by now. Eva wanted me to have her send over two 'perfect' red roses tied with trailing lavender ribbons. She's had the brainstorm that she and poor Nancy should carry those down the aisle as they're escorted to their seats."

Bonnie was obviously dissatisfied by the abrupt change of subject, but she had to agree this was the wrong time for a heart-to-heart conversation. She gave a light squeeze to Kinley's arm, a gesture of support and affection, then moved toward the doorway. "I have a lot to do myself. Good luck dealing with Eva today.

It would probably be better for our future business if you refrain yourself from strangling her prior to the wedding."

Kinley forced a laugh. "I'll do my best."

Dan made an effort to stay in the background and out of the way Saturday. He found it interesting how much work went on behind-the-scenes in preparation for an outdoor wedding. A simple justice-of-the-peace courthouse wedding sounded better to him all the time—if he should ever find himself in a position of wanting to be married, of course.

Perhaps coincidentally—or maybe not—he searched out Kinley in the controlled chaos. She'd been bustling around all day, usually with her phone to her ear or at her fingertips as she scrolled and texted. When she wasn't on the phone, she was deep in consultation with one of the wedding subcontractors, or mingling with her warm hostess smile among guests of the inn. All six of the other suites were currently occupied but he'd gleaned that four of the suites would be empty after the wedding tonight. While he was sure the Carmichaels preferred a full inn, he'd bet they would appreciate a slow day or two to recuperate from this particular event.

He had confirmed with Bonnie that his own suite was available for an extra night or two. Though he'd planned originally to leave immediately after the wedding, he couldn't say now exactly when he would move on. Bonnie had made no comment in response to his request other than to say he was welcome to stay as long as he liked, but he wondered if she was aware that her sister was the reason he was in no hurry to check out.

Kinley had greeted him pleasantly enough when

she'd first seen him earlier, her expression so well schooled that he doubted any observer would have suspected there were any simmering undertones between them. She looked far more composed and controlled than the passionate woman who'd burned in his arms only hours earlier. The contrast between those two sides of her fascinated him, but then, so did just about everything else about her. Even the things that—as she'd phrased it—pushed his buttons.

Eva had decided that no guests should be out in the garden between two and four that afternoon, which was when she had instructed all final touches should be added to the decorations. Any guests who arrived for the five o'clock ceremony before four should mingle inside the inn, she'd proclaimed. That way everything would be in place to perfection when the ushers started the seating.

Dan exempted himself from those instructions because he didn't consider himself a guest of the wedding. He wandered outside at three, idly watching as the garden became a hive of eleventh-hour activity. He'd thought the place was fully decorated the night before, but he saw now that there'd been plenty of touches held in reserve for the wedding itself. Baskets of flowers that perhaps wouldn't have held up all night, fresh white candles in the fancy wrought iron holders, straightening of bows and garlands ruffled by overnight breezes. He smiled when he saw Logan raking the pebbled aisle path, smoothing the small white rocks and removing any leaves and twigs.

"Quite a production, isn't it?" he asked as he approached Kinley's brother.

Logan leaned on the handle of the rake and nodded,

his politely affable expression doing little to soften the hard lines of his face. "Some more so than others," he said. "This is one of the more-sos."

"Need any help?"

"No, we've got it. There's not really anything left to do, but we're trying to look busy to keep Mrs. Sossaman from thinking up some new instructions for us."

Dan chuckled. "Understandable."

Logan glanced toward Dan's cheek. "That looks sore."

"Looks worse than it is. Just a scratch."

"Get it last night? Looking for the kid?"

"Yeah. Slapped in the face by a branch."

Logan nodded. "The kid's a holy terror. Being around him makes me doubly glad I never had any."

Dan remembered Bonnie's carefully worded comment that her brother had been betrayed in love. He was curious, of course, but aware that the details were none of his business. He directed the conversation into a less sensitive direction. "That's quite a dog you've got. Smart."

"Sneaky," Logan corrected with a shake of his head and a crooked smile. "I had no idea he'd learned to open the gate until Kinley told me last night. I took care of it, of course, but he'll probably figure out the combination to the lock soon enough."

Laughing, Dan nodded. "I wouldn't be surprised. I like him."

"Yeah, me, too. Kinley's been hinting that I should find another home for him, but I'm not giving him up. You could say we've bonded."

Dan couldn't imagine Kinley would really insist that her brother give up the pet he'd grown attached to, though he didn't blame her for wanting the deceptively intimidating-looking dog kept away from unsuspecting guests. "Last night was the first time I'd heard him bark."

Logan shrugged. "I've never heard him, myself. Guess he just hasn't had a reason to bark until then."

Pushing his hands into his pockets, Dan cleared his throat. "So…you've lived in the caretaker's cottage for a couple years now, right?"

Logan looked automatically in that direction. "Yeah. I like it. Being down in the woods gives me plenty of privacy, considering I'm right on the grounds of the inn."

"I, uh, guess you know these woods pretty well by now."

"Well enough." Logan eyed him as if wondering where this line of questioning was leading.

"Ever go out walking at night?"

"I've been known to."

Dan worried a loose pebble with the toe of his shoe. "Ever see anything, well, strange out there?"

Logan cocked his dark head, his expression quizzical. "What was it you thought you saw?"

"I'm not sure, exactly," Dan admitted. "Something. I think Kinley saw it, too, but she won't admit it."

"Don't tell me you think you saw the ghost." Logan's sudden scowl reminded Dan very much of Kinley. It was the first time he'd seen such a strong resemblance between them. "You should know I don't believe in that nonsense. And I agree with Kinley that I don't want to turn the inn into some sort of haunted-house attraction."

Dan nodded to acknowledge that he'd gotten the message. He started to speak but was interrupted by a hail from the direction of the inn.

"Logan, there you are!" Eva bustled toward them, the sun catching on the sparkles in the silver threads of her lavender suit.

Logan groaned beneath his breath, but asked politely enough, "What can I do for you, Mrs. Sossaman?"

"I just wanted to make sure you smoothed that rough patch at the end of the path by the gazebo. I would hate for anyone in the wedding party to trip during the procession. Serena would be devastated."

"If you're talking about that hole Grayson dug looking for worms, then yes, I filled it in and smoothed it out," Logan said with a curt nod.

"Good. Dan, have you found where you're going to stand to take pictures of the wedding? I was thinking if you stood right there on the east corner of the deck that you'd have a nice overview of the decorations and the gazebo. You should take several, of course, but especially while Serena and Chris are facing each other reciting their vows, so their faces will be in the photos. I'll be sure and send you some of the professional photos if you'll leave me your email address, but I assume you'll want to take a few of your own."

"I'll handle it," he assured her. "You'll never even know I'm here."

Especially since he had no intention of staying for the whole ceremony. He could slip away after snapping a perfunctory shot or two and no one would be the wiser.

Leaving Logan to his preparations, he moved toward the inn, thinking he'd go up to his room and work on some notes for a while. Maybe concentrating on work would keep him from dwelling on thoughts of Kinley—or of unexplained visions in the woods surrounding her inn.

At four on the dot, Kinley and Bonnie opened the back doors to the inn for those inside who wanted to go on out and be seated. Later arrivals would be welcome to come through the inn or go around straight from the parking lot to be seated. Tables were already set up beneath the tent on the side lawn for the meal to follow the ceremony, and the catering crew bustled around in the kitchen, getting ready to serve.

The inn did not provide a specific dressing room for the groom and groomsmen; usually they made use of one of the suites, either reserved for the purpose or borrowed from a guest. The bride and her bridesmaids were allowed to use the downstairs guest restroom for dressing. It was a decent size, with a sink-and-dressing area separate from the enclosed toilet. It was one of Kinley's goals to someday convert the unused part of the basement below the deck into restroom/dressing room areas accessible from outside, one for men and one for women.

Serena and her three bridesmaids bustled in and out of the restroom while Eva badgered them to hurry. The photographer had asked the wedding party to meet in the parlor promptly at four for a session of posed photos in front of the fireplace. Serena and Chris would join them there, since Serena had insisted she didn't mind Chris seeing her in her gown prior to the ceremony. At ten past four, everyone was gathered in the parlor except Serena. With Eva hovering around the edges making suggestions, the long-suffering photographer,

Anne Saxon, arranged the groom with his groomsmen for several poses, then took a few shots of the groom with the bridesmaids.

Serena sent out word that she needed a few minutes alone to calm herself for the wedding. Eva went to check on her, but was sent back to the parlor with a frown that she tried to smooth over. Eva fidgeted restlessly while the groom's family was the center of the photographer's focus as they waited for the bride to join them. Anne posed Chris with his parents, his brother and sister-in-law and their three boys, then took a couple of cute shots of Chris solemnly entrusting the rings into Grayson's care. Kinley was relieved to note that the rings immediately went into Chris's brother's pocket afterward; as best man, he would guard the rings while Grayson served only as a symbolic ring bearer.

"The boy looks deceptively angelic in photos, doesn't he?" a deep voice murmured into Kinley's ear. For a heart-stopping moment, she was transported back into her darkened bedroom with that same husky voice whispering intimate encouragements to her. She shoved the memories immediately to the back of her mind, knowing she would pull them out later to replay in detail.

Smiling blandly up at Dan, she nodded and murmured, "He does. He's been very well behaved today. I think he got quite a talking-to last night, and probably this morning."

His hand brushed hers at her side. It was a fleeting touch that might have almost been accidental, but she knew it wasn't. A little tingle of reaction coursed from that whisper of contact all the way through her. She moistened her lips and tried to concentrate on the wedding preparations.

At four-thirty, Serena still had not made an appearance. Eva started in that direction, but her forbidding expression made Kinley move quickly to block her.

"Would you like me to bring her?" she offered brightly, hoping to avoid what looked as if it could become a noisy confrontation. "Perhaps you'd like a photo of yourself with the ring bearer and flower girl? That would be a sweet memento."

Reluctantly distracted, Eva nodded. "I would like that. Anne, maybe I could sit in that chair in front of the window with the lace curtains behind me while the children hand me flowers. That would be sweet, wouldn't it? Someone bring us flowers to use."

"I'll find some," Alicia said, giving Kinley a nod of approval as she passed her. "Tell Serena there's going to be a maternal meltdown if she doesn't get out here," she murmured from the corner of her mouth on the way by.

Maybe Dan was reluctant to be left in the same room as Eva without Kinley there as a shield. He followed her, leaning against the hallway wall some distance away when she tapped lightly on the restroom door, not really eavesdropping but just waiting for her.

"Serena? It's Kinley. How are you doing in there?"

"I just need some time, okay?"

Kinley winced a little at the edge she heard in the younger woman's voice even through the wood door. Was that just a hint of hysteria? "Serena, your family is waiting for you. They'd like to take a few photos with you before the ceremony starts, and there's not much time left."

The door was jerked open and Serena stood framed in the opening, her furious expression a startling contrast to her angelic appearance. Her strapless dress

was a poufy confection of ruffles and lace wrapped
with a wide lavender ribbon tied in a big bow in back.
Her stiffly upswept hair was framed by a full white
veil anchored with a rhinestone-studded tiara. The en-
semble was much too froufrou for Kinley's personal
taste, but she had to admit Serena looked very pretty—
except for the streaks of tears through the makeup on
her flushed cheeks.

"Why won't you all just leave me alone?" she wailed,
her fists clenched at her sides. "I said I needed some
time to myself."

Kinley had dealt with a couple of overwhelmed
brides by now, and she'd found that a calm, soothing
tone worked best. "I understand, Serena. I'm sure you're
exhausted from all the preparations. It's almost over.
If you'll just—"

"You." Serena almost spat out the word. "You're as
bad as my mother with your schedules and checklists
and wanting everything to be just so. You'll probably
be just like her in a few years. Telling everyone what
to do, pushing them around."

Kinley bit her lower lip, telling herself it was foolish
to be hurt by Serena's angry words. Obviously the bride
wasn't thinking clearly, was simply lashing out at the
closest target. She sensed Dan moving slowly closer, but
she held up a hand to warn him off as she spoke again.

"I'm not trying to tell you what to do, Serena. Why
don't you tell me what you want me to do? Should I
inform everyone there will be a short delay, that the
wedding will start a bit later than planned? You should
take all the time you need to compose yourself, but I
need to let them know not to start the ceremony until
you're ready."

"I don't know when I'll be ready," Serena snapped. "Maybe I don't want to do this at all. Maybe I just want to call the whole thing off."

Swallowing hard, Kinley shot a quick, rather panicked look at Dan before turning back to Serena. "That's your call, too, of course," she said evenly. "By all means, if you've changed your mind about marrying Chris, now is the time to say so."

Tears cascaded again. "I don't know. It's all just so—"

"So what?" Kinley encouraged.

"It's all my mother," Serena whispered miserably. "Everything. The decorations, the menu, the music. This stupid, frilly dress that makes me look like an idiot. I let her railroad me into every decision so there wouldn't be a fight, and now I hate it. I hate it all."

"And me?" Chris appeared suddenly from behind Dan, his plain face somber. "Do you hate me, too?"

Serena looked at him with wide, shocked eyes, then burst into tears again.

Out of the corner of her eye, Kinley saw Bonnie guarding the end of the doorway, refusing to allow anyone past. Especially the mother of the bride. "Everyone just go back to the parlor," Bonnie said firmly. "The bride will be with you when she's ready. Mr. Sossaman?"

Taking the cue, Clinton stepped forward to take his wife's arm. "Let's go back to the parlor, dear. Actually, I wouldn't mind a photo of just the two of us. When's the last time we had our picture taken, hmm? Anne, you wouldn't mind that, would you?"

The voices faded away, leaving Chris and Serena, Kinley and Dan in the hallway. Kinley started to move away, but Serena grabbed her arm, changing from attack mode to clinging. "I don't know what to do," the frantic bride choked.

"What do you *want* to do?" Kinley asked, at a loss as to how to proceed.

"I love you, Serena," Chris said huskily. "I want to marry you. But if you want to stop everything right now, we'll stop. I don't care what your mother says, or my mother or anyone else. You're all that matters to me."

Serena's breath caught in a hitch as fresh tears leaked from her red-rimmed eyes. She looked from her fiancé to Kinley, as if hoping now that someone would tell her what to do despite her earlier resistance. Perhaps she did want that. Having been raised by Eva, Serena wasn't accustomed to making her own decisions.

"I can't tell you what's best for you," Kinley said simply. "I can take care of everything if you choose to call it off, or I can keep everything on hold while you make up your mind. But ultimately, the call is yours to make."

Letting a long, unsteady sigh escape her, Serena sagged. "I love you," she said to Chris. "I want to marry you. I just wish I'd stood up to her more, so that the wedding would reflect *us*. Not her."

Now Kinley felt more certain. She wasn't confident about calming hysterical young women, but she knew how to take charge when necessary. "What do you want to change?" she asked briskly. "Tell me, and we'll take care of it, if at all possible."

Serena stared at her wide-eyed. "What?"

Taking out her phone, Kinley opened her checklist. "Some things are a little too far along to change, of course. The menu, for example. I'm afraid that's set. But if it makes you feel better, it all sounds delicious.

I'm sure your guests will enjoy the meal. The ceremony itself hasn't started yet. We can hold the guests in their seats, maybe play some music or something to entertain them while you make any adjustments you want. I'll call the musicians and soloist and you can discuss musical selections. Maybe they'll have music you prefer in their repertoires. My friend Janelle owns the bridal shop where you got your dress. The shop is open until six. I'm sure I can convince her to send over a selection of dresses in your size. Or I could send someone to pick them up. Logan would probably go."

"You would do that?" Serena seemed stunned. "Change things at the last minute like this?"

"It's your wedding," Kinley reminded her. "My job is just to get things done the way you want them. I have sort of a knack for making things happen."

Grimacing, Serena murmured, "About what I said earlier—"

Kinley brushed off the impending apology. "What do you want to do?"

Squaring her shoulders, the young woman looked at her groom, then nodded decisively. "I want to get married."

She reached up to take hold of the rhinestone tiara and tug it from her hair. "And I don't want to wear this stupid veil. Or this ridiculous bow. Maybe we can work with the rest of it."

Chris grinned, relief making him look a little giddy when he said, "If you'll excuse me, I'm going to go out to speak to the soloist. She's my cousin, after all. I've heard her sing more times than I can even remember. And I happen to know she's very versatile. Just like the pianist—her husband."

Serena caught her breath, clasping her hands in front of her. "Remember that song they did at Gabrielle and Bobby's engagement party? The Lady Antebellum one we loved but Mom hated? She said it didn't sound like a wedding song, even though I told her I didn't care about that. And maybe I don't have to enter to Mendelssohn? You know I really wanted Pachelbel, even though Mom said it's overdone. Like the traditional wedding march isn't," she added with an exasperated shake of her head.

Chris stepped forward to press a hard kiss to his bride's mouth. "I'll take care of it," he said huskily. "See you at the altar. Just let me know when you're ready."

"I'll send you a signal," Kinley promised.

Taking the reins and running now, Serena called out to Bonnie. "Tell Anne we'll take pictures with me in them after the ceremony, while the other guests are being seated for the meal. I'll apologize to the wedding party for inconveniencing them, but there's no need to delay the ceremony any longer. I should be ready by a quarter after five or so."

"How can I help?" Dan asked.

"If you want to help, stay close," Kinley replied. "I may need you to help me get everyone in place when Serena's ready."

"I'd be delighted." Dan glanced at Serena. "It's going to be a beautiful wedding," he assured her. "Your fiancé is a lucky man."

Swiping at her damp cheeks with the back of one hand, smearing her makeup even worse, Serena managed a shaky smile. "Thank you."

Kinley rested a hand on Serena's shoulder. "Let's go freshen your makeup and get rid of that bow, shall we?"

Gratefully, Serena nodded and turned to precede

Kinley into the dressing room. Telling herself she would be supremely grateful when this day was over, Kinley glanced again at Dan, then followed Serena to see what they could do about the too-frilly wedding dress.

The ceremony started only twenty minutes late. The groom and his groomsmen, given the signal by Dan, took their places on the raised gazebo floor. The ring bearer, bridesmaids and flower girl proceeded toward them from the inn while the pianist played *Pachelbel's Canon in D.* Her hair brushed into a soft, shiny curtain around her shoulders, adorned with a simple white flower clipped above one ear, her face glowing with only a touch of natural-looking makeup, the bride came down the path on her father's arm. Her strapless dress was still a little poufy, but looked somewhat more streamlined without the lavender sash and bow.

The soloist sang "Just A Kiss." The nontraditional song made some of the older ladies raise their eyebrows in surprise, but Chris and Serena gazed at each other in visible delight during the rendition. Kinley found herself getting lost in the lyrics about a kiss in the moonlight leading to a potential lifelong partnership.

"Be the one I've been waiting for my whole life." Something about those words made her heart contract with what felt suspiciously like fear.

She peeked toward the woods beyond the gazebo and swallowed hard. Then glanced at Dan, who leaned against the railing of the deck above her. He was there ostensibly to take photos, but when she looked up at him, she found him gazing back down at her. Their eyes held for several beats of the romantic song, but then she made herself turn away.

She had a job to do, she reminded herself. It wasn't like her to let anything, or anyone, get in the way of that. She would probably have to remind herself again before this night was over.

Chapter Ten

Several hours later, Kinley sat in her sister's living room, sipping a glass of wine and wondering where she was going to find the energy to drive herself home. Maybe she'd just crash in Bonnie's spare room. It wouldn't be the first time. And if she did that, she would definitely be the only one in the bed, she thought, looking at Dan through her lashes over the rim of her glass. Bonnie had invited him to join them in their traditional after-event celebration, which usually consisted of a glass of wine each while they sprawled wearily on Bonnie's furniture.

"I can't believe how close we came to total disaster today," Bonnie groaned from her armchair. "Can you imagine if Serena had really called off the wedding right before it started?"

Logan shook his head incredulously. "With all that planning and expense and trouble, you'd think she'd have had the guts to tell her mother sooner what she wanted in her wedding."

"Her mother's a scary woman," Dan said with a chuckle. "But I have to say I'd never seen her as quiet as she was after the wedding. I think Serena's rebellion knocked her for a loop. For once, Eva was at a loss for words."

"Here's to Eva Sossaman being at a loss for words," Logan said gravely, raising his glass.

Everyone sipped along with him.

"And you." Dan nodded toward Kinley. "Were you really prepared to restructure the whole wedding half an hour before it started, right down to the bride's dress?"

She shrugged ironically. "If I'd had to. I was taking a bit of a calculated risk, though. I hoped that if she felt as if she had a choice, Serena would leave most everything in place. I know her mother railroaded her into some of the choices, but I was there when quite a few of the decisions were made, and Serena had a little more input than she let on. She's the one who wanted lavender and white for her colors, and she made a few suggestions to the menu that her mother approved. Once she'd made a few minor changes, she was calm enough to go on with the ceremony."

Dan smiled wryly. "So basically she turned a case of bridal jitters into an all-out rebellion against her mother."

"Basically."

"So, do we really want to keep specializing in weddings?" Logan asked with his dry humor. "Maybe we should switch to hosting fiftieth wedding anniversaries. Catering to nice, sane older couples rather than hysterical brides and meddling mamas."

"We love hosting weddings," Kinley asserted firmly, pointing a finger at Dan. "Be sure you make that clear in the article. Everything you've heard us say in private family quarters is off the record."

He grinned. "I wouldn't dare betray your confidences. Your brother would probably sic Ninja on me."

"I'd be more worried about Kinley than Ninja," Logan muttered before setting his empty wineglass aside. "I'm heading home. I'll be out early in the morning taking down the rest of the wedding stuff."

Many of the decorations had been removed during the leisurely wedding dinner. The florist's crew had hauled away rented accoutrement, the musicians had packed up the keyboard and sound equipment and Logan and Zach had swiftly folded and stacked chairs. Soft background music for the dinner had been piped from speakers discreetly installed on the side lawn. The elaborate cake had been cut, toasts made, bouquet thrown. For guests interested in dancing and drinking, the party had then moved to a nearby club where a live band and an open bar would be provided for their entertainment beginning at eight o'clock and going quite late. Though she hadn't been involved in the planning for that part of the celebration, Kinley had heard that there would be a two-free-drink limit at the bar. Probably a good idea, considering everything else that had happened that afternoon.

"Do you have a wedding next weekend?" Dan asked.

"A very simple one Sunday afternoon," Bonnie replied. "Only two attendants and thirty guests, a few candles and flowers for decorations and hors d'oeuvres and wedding cake afterward rather than a meal."

"That sounds more to my taste," he remarked.

"Does it?" Bonnie looked with a smile from Dan to Kinley, who frowned at her playful sister.

Ignoring her, Bonnie spoke again to Dan. "I'm glad you could stay with us an extra night. Do you have plans for tomorrow?"

"I was hoping I could talk your sister into showing me some of the local attractions," he replied, looking at Kinley as he spoke. "Someone told me there's an observation tower that's fun to visit. A few historic buildings that might be interesting to tour."

Aware that her siblings' eyes had turned to focus on her, Kinley shifted in her seat. "Well, I do have some paperwork to take care of tomorrow."

"For pity's sake, Kinley, you can take a Sunday afternoon off," Bonnie said with open exasperation. "You even made Logan stay out for a while Friday evening because you said he'd been working too hard and needed a few hours away from the inn."

"You did say that," Logan agreed placidly, seeming to enjoy her discomfiture.

"You could think of showing me around as part of your marketing job," Dan suggested, then grinned. "But I'd actually rather you didn't."

"Fine," she said with a bit less grace than she would have liked. "You want to climb a tower, we'll climb a tower. But you'd better wear comfortable shoes. It's a two hundred step climb and it's windy at the top."

He smiled in satisfaction. "Sounds great."

"Be sure and have some of the fudge in the country store," Logan said as he carried his wineglass to the sink then headed for the door. "My favorite is the maple."

"I'll keep that in mind, thanks."

Kinley pushed a hand through her hair. "I should go,

too. It's been a long day." Especially considering how little sleep she'd had the night before, though of course she kept that thought to herself.

Dan set his glass beside hers. "I'll walk you to your car. We'll make our plans for tomorrow."

She nodded, bade good-night to her sister, then grabbed her bulging tote bag and walked outside with Dan.

It seemed as if a very long time had passed since she'd parked at the side of the inn that morning. So much had happened that day. Muscles already sore from her fall in the woods ached a bit with weariness now. She considered herself to be in good physical condition, but the events of the past thirty-six hours had been enough to exhaust anyone, she assured herself.

It was fully dark out now, of course. Soft lighting illuminated the walkway to her car. With most of the guests away at the wedding dance, it was quiet in the gardens, the sounds of the big fountain drifting through the cool air. Their footsteps crunched on the gravel path. An owl hooted somewhere in the woods, but Kinley didn't look in that direction. Not that she expected to see anything, of course. She was simply focused on her destination, her keys already in hand.

Pressing the remote button to unlock her door, she looked up at Dan when they reached her car. "So... sightseeing tomorrow."

He chuckled and ran a hand slowly up her arm. "I sort of put you on the spot in there, didn't I? I'd apologize— but since it worked, I can't really say I'm sorry."

She laughed. "At least you're honest."

"Always," he assured her with a smile that gleamed in the shadows.

She focused on those smiling lips, vividly remembering the taste of them, the feel of them against her most sensitive skin. Muscles tightened low in her abdomen, and her fingers clenched reflexively around her key fob.

Dan's smile faded as he read the expressions crossing her face. He shifted closer to her, lowering his head to speak close to her lips. "I can honestly say that last night was spectacular," he murmured. "Incredible. And I'm sorely tempted to ask you now if I could follow you home. The only reason I'm resisting that urge is because I think you need some time to yourself tonight."

"If you asked, I'd be sorely tempted to say yes," she whispered, resting her free hand on his chest, feeling his heart beating rapidly beneath his shirt. "But you're right, I think. I could use a little time to recuperate from today."

Not to mention space to clear her head, to reinforce the barricades around her wary heart. For the past few days, she'd been bombarded by emotions from all directions, all framed within the trappings of romance and fantasy. Maybe that affected the intense feelings she'd developed toward Dan. Maybe a good night's sleep—alone—would help her enjoy her time with him tomorrow without reading too much into every touch, every smile. Without leaving her bereft when it inevitably ended.

His faint sigh expressed his regret with their decision. He took her lips in a thorough kiss that might have been intended to hold them over until tomorrow. She wasn't sure she would ever get her fill of Dan's kisses, but she'd enjoy what she could get, she assured herself, taking her time kissing him back.

When at last he raised his head, he had her face

cupped in both his hands. "Really tempted," he muttered.

She bit her lip to hold back the invitation that hovered on her tongue. Dan stepped back before it could escape despite her.

"Good night, Kinley. Drive carefully. I'll see you tomorrow."

She nodded. "I'll be here in the morning for Sunday brunch. I'll see you then."

"I'll count the minutes," he assured her. His tone was teasing, but she thought the words were true, anyway—at least as far as she was concerned. Which didn't bode well for her common sense returning any time soon when it came to Dan Phelan.

"You were right about the wind." Dan braced himself against the railing at the top of the slightly swaying metal observation tower as he smiled down at Kinley, his hair whipping around his face. "It's pretty strong up here. But the view is spectacular."

The Big Walker Lookout Tower soared a hundred feet high at an elevation of just over thirty-four hundred feet, so the air was thin but the view really was worth the strenuous climb. On a clear day like this one, mountain peaks in five different states were visible from their vantage point. Spreading below them to the north was a patchwork network of farmland. To the south, the dense Jefferson National Forest spread like a thick green blanket almost as far as they could see. A big hawk circled lazily nearby, riding the currents and keeping an eye out below for lunch. Kinley enjoyed watching birds, but she hadn't yet taken time to learn to identify different types, so she had no idea what kind of hawk it was. Someday she was going to spend more free time birding and learning, she promised herself.

"You should visit in the fall," she said, the stiff breeze whipping the words from her mouth. "The colors in the forest are breathtaking when viewed from here."

"I'll bet." Like the few other tourists at the top with them, Dan lifted his camera to try to capture the magic in pixels. Having taken photos from there quite a few times herself, Kinley knew there was no way to really reduce the majesty of the scene to a snapshot. She'd seen some beautiful shots, but nothing compared to being up there surrounded by the beauty that was Virginia.

"I can see why you wanted to make your home here," Dan said as if he'd read her thoughts. "It's really beautiful countryside. Nice people. Lots of nature to enjoy."

She nodded. "I love hiking the mountain trails when I have a few hours off work. There's a whole network of excellent trails around this area."

"And when's the last time you made use of one of those trails?"

She cleared her throat, trying to remember the last time she'd taken a few hours just to enjoy a trail. She'd hardly even broken in the new hiking boots she'd bought on sale last fall. Perhaps she had needed this outing today. Though a list of work-related things she needed to attend to whispered at the back of her mind, she ignored them and allowed herself to savor the lovely view—not to mention the very nice companionship.

"It's, um, been a while," she admitted.

Dan shook his head and stroked a wind-whipped strand of hair from her face. "Life's too short to spend it all working, Kinley. There are so many more interesting things to do."

Feeling the sting of old wounds, she shrugged and replied with a somewhat brittle tone, "Not if I want to make a lasting success of an inn that was out of business for eighteen years."

He lifted an eyebrow. "Just you? I thought your brother and sister were equally invested in that goal."

She didn't really have a response to that comment. "Are you ready to head back down? You said you wanted to spend some time wandering through the general store."

The look he gave her let her know he was aware of her prevarication, but he didn't push it. "First, I'll steal a kiss here at the top of the world," he murmured with a smile.

She let him steal more than one, despite the few other people up there with them, none of whom seemed to be interested in her and Dan.

Releasing her before they embarrassed themselves, Dan took one final look around the perimeter of the tower, snapped a few more photos and then started down the winding stairs with her.

The original general store building had burned more than a decade earlier and had been rebuilt close to the old site. A long swinging bridge over the parking lot had once connected the tower to the old store. The bridge was still accessible for adventurous visitors, and Dan of course insisted on crossing it with her, laughing as the structure swayed in the wind.

A bluegrass trio played on the porch of the store, which was designed to look old and weathered. Inside, the shelves were lined with jams, jellies, relishes and other vintage food items, in addition to homemade candies, local craft items and a big assortment of souvenirs. Dan made a beeline for the ice cream parlor where he ordered a double scoop of mint-chocolate chip in a waffle cone. Kinley requested one scoop of peach ice cream in a paper cup.

"You can indulge more than that," Dan teased her. "Especially after climbing the steps to the top of the tower."

"No, this is plenty," she assured him primly. Then added with a grin, "Besides, I'm buying half a pound of fudge on my way out."

She would share the candy with her siblings. Maybe. But she wasn't leaving this place without fudge.

They sat outside at a picnic table for a while to enjoy the music and watch tourists crossing the swinging bridge and climbing the tower. Having made short work of the ice cream, Dan sneaked bites of the fudge he'd bought for himself. "What can I say?" he asked when she teased him about it. "Climbing steps makes me hungry."

Judging by how fit he was, he climbed enough steps to offset the calories, she thought with a wistful sigh.

He'd hardly touched her today other than those kisses at the top of the tower—and yet the physical awareness had sizzled between them all day, just beneath the surface of their smiles and conversation. She suspected it would always be this way for her when Dan was around. Which, she reminded herself firmly, would not be much longer.

"Where do you go next?" she asked somewhat abruptly. "Your next assignment, I mean?"

"I have a couple of options. A series of profiles of Southern beach resorts along the Atlantic and Gulf Coasts. Another about the best places that serve Southern fried pies. I have a fondness for chocolate fried pies, myself."

"So, you have a choice of lolling on beaches or stuffing yourself with fried pies. Tough call."

He chuckled. "Maybe I should do a series on the best fried pies to be found in beach resorts."

Kinley rubbed her thumb over the case of her cell phone. She'd silenced the ringer and had only glanced at the screen when a vibration signaled an incoming call or text, just to make sure she wasn't missing anything important by putting off her responses until later. Fortunately there hadn't been many calls, since it was a Sunday. "What about your story idea? Your friend the producer who wants to see a treatment? Are you going to send him anything?"

"Maybe. Eventually."

She bit her lip.

Dan sighed and closed his bag of fudge with a noisy crinkle. "It's all you can do not to give me a lecture about wasting my potential, isn't it? Trust me, I've heard it. My cousin pulls it out every so often. My parents have given up trying. They don't say much of anything to me anymore—not that Dad remembers who I am half the time, anyway."

Kinley grimaced. "I'm sorry. Alzheimer's?"

Keeping his gaze on the bluegrass trio, Dan shrugged. "Yeah. My folks were classic overachievers. You'd have identified with them, I think. Mom taught pharmacology at the University of Alabama School of Medicine, Dad was a law professor at Cumberland School of Law."

"I see." She couldn't think of anything else to say, though she wondered if that had been a dig about her identifying with his parents. She was pretty sure it had been.

"Anyway, they wanted me to be a doctor or a lawyer. They would have settled for a pharmacist or a dentist, though they wouldn't have been particularly happy about either. A journalism degree was one of the last options they'd have picked for me. The military wasn't even on their list of acceptable possibilities."

Kinley remembered that he'd mentioned his parents had usually left him in the care of nannies rather than taking care of him, themselves. Had he bucked their wishes when it came to career choices as a form of rebellion? Or maybe in an attempt to get their attention? Whichever, it was sad.

"Is that why you moved back to Alabama to work with your cousin?" she asked tentatively. "Because of your father's condition?"

After a momentary hesitation, he nodded. "I had the idea that maybe my mother would need me. I was wrong, of course. She hired sitters for him and went on with her life. Pretty much the same way she approached motherhood. Which is why I feel no real obligation to stay in Hoover much longer. I'm sure my cousin will be able to replace me at the magazine."

"Do you ever see your parents?"

"Oh, sure. We have dinner occasionally. Very civil. Mom assures me that there's still time for me to go back to law school, though she reminds me occasionally that I'm not getting any younger. Dad tells me stories about his glory days as a distinguished professor and about some of the renowned politicians who passed through his classes. He remembers those people. It's his son he's forgotten."

"I'm sorry, Dan," she said quietly.

He grunted and pushed a hand through his hair. "No, I'm sorry. Talking about my folks makes me grumpy. Let's just leave it that they aren't particularly happy with the way I'm living."

"Are *you?*" she couldn't resist asking. "Or are you still trying to prove to them that you can do what you want?"

He stood, tossed a crumpled paper napkin into a trash bin and turned toward the car. "Ready to move on?"

"Yes." She rose, too, wondering if a metaphor was buried in his question or if she was simply overthinking his words. "I suppose we should."

By unspoken agreement, they headed straight back to the inn after leaving the general store. They were in Kinley's car, and she drove the scenic route back. She mentioned specific hiking trails they passed along the way, some that led to waterfalls or picnic areas or awe-inspiring overlooks, but they didn't stop again. Dan was rather quiet during the drive, admiring the views she pointed out, responding courteously when she spoke, but distant in a way that he had not been before.

They didn't talk about his parents again, or her work, or anything that had taken place between them—kisses or lovemaking or shared illusions in the fog. Something had changed between them during that conversation at the picnic table, and Kinley didn't understand it. But she felt it.

She parked in her usual place toward the back of the inn and they climbed out of the car. Dan closed his door, then glanced around the garden. No one seemed to be around at the moment, which was no surprise. Few of the rooms were occupied now that the wedding party had moved out, and it was time for the light Sunday supper to be served inside, so the guests in residence were probably in the dining room.

"Bonnie sets out a simple meal at this time on Sunday evenings," she said to Dan, more to make conversation than because he didn't already know. "A big pot of soup, sandwich makings, desserts. You've got almost an hour before it's all put away."

"I'm not really hungry. Too many sweets, I guess. Maybe we could walk in the garden for a few minutes?"

"Of course."

She noticed as they strolled in silence toward the fountain that all evidence of the wedding had been stashed away. The gardens and lawn were immaculate as always, the gazebo decorated with pots of leafy ferns rather than baskets of wedding flowers. Her brother was always fast and thorough with the chores he had claimed as his own. She wished she believed he was genuinely happy with his life now.

Reaching the fountain, Dan stopped to gaze down into the rippling pool, studying the shiny handful of coins there as if totaling their value. She wasn't sure he was even seeing the change. It seemed to her that he was thinking hard about what he was about to say, and she braced herself to hear it.

"I think I'll check out this evening," he said. "I'm considering driving over to Chesapeake Bay. My assignment here is finished, and I'm sure you have a busy week ahead."

Somehow she'd sensed this was what he was going to say, but it made it no easier to hear it. She wasn't sure what, exactly, had brought him to this decision.

What she'd said—or hadn't said. Why he suddenly felt the urge to cut his losses and move on. She wouldn't ask him to stay. After all, this was the outcome she had expected all along. She was strongly rooted here, furiously busy with the inn and the part-time real-estate job she'd been neglecting the past couple of days. Dan wasn't rooted anywhere, admitting that he preferred being free to move at will, apparently averse to making any binding plans for his future. Whether that was the way he truly preferred to live or whether he would spend the rest of his life rebelling against parental expectations, she didn't know—but there was no place for her in that existence, either way.

"I'll let Bonnie know," she said, pleased that her voice sounded so steady. "She'll check you out."

He was silent for several long beats, still staring down into the water. Had he expected her to argue? Had he wanted her to?

"I've had a great time," he said at length, turning to her with his expression carefully schooled to reveal little of his thoughts. The scratch on his cheek stood out against his tan, a visible reminder of the adventure they had shared and which she, for one, would never forget.

"I had fun, too," she assured him, and that part was surprisingly true. It had been fun being with Dan, for the most part. Perhaps that would help buffer the pain of missing him later.

He reached out to smooth her hair, a gesture she was going to miss whenever she thought of him—which she was sure she would do often. "If you were the type to ditch all those responsibilities and take off for some fun in the sun, I'd ask you to come with me."

Her smile felt a bit sad even to her. "If you were the

type to buckle down to all those responsibilities and
be content with only a few rare hours of relaxation, I'd
ask you to stay."

His mouth twitched. "That doesn't really describe
either of us, does it?"

"No."

Cupping her face in his hands, he kissed her linger-
ingly. She closed her eyes and sank into his embrace,
returning the kiss, committing the feel and taste and
scent of him to memory for savoring later. He tilted his
head, kissed her again, then seemed to force himself
to draw away.

"I hope your inn is as successful as you want it to
be," he murmured when he released her.

"And I hope you find whatever it is you're looking
for," she replied huskily.

She couldn't stay there any longer. The one thing
she absolutely refused to do was to cry in front of him.
"Goodbye, Dan."

"Bye, Kinley. I—"

Whatever he might have added, he bit it off. She was
already walking away, heading almost blindly down the
path past the gazebo. She wasn't sure why she'd chosen
to come this way, but she didn't reverse her steps. She
kept walking, her eyes focused fiercely on the caretaker's cottage, looking neither behind her at Dan nor to
the side at the once-so-familiar, now-mysterious woods.

Reaching her brother's door, she rapped hard with
her knuckles. She didn't even know for certain if he
was inside, but she thought she heard a ball game on
his TV. The door opened, and Logan stood inside, casual in a T-shirt and jeans with bare feet, frowning at
the interruption.

The frown changed when he saw her face.

"Can I come in?" she asked.

He stepped aside silently. She walked past him, waited until he'd closed the door and then buried her face in his shoulder. Sprawled on the floor by the couch, Ninja raised his head, then lowered it to his paws again as though sensing the siblings needed to be left alone for the moment.

Logan sighed and wrapped his arms around her. "Want me to go pound the guy?"

With a watery laugh, she shook her head against his chest. "No. But thanks for the offer."

"Want a sandwich and a beer? We can watch the rest of the game together."

Filling her lungs unsteadily, she pulled herself together and straightened, telling herself she was back in control now. "Yes, please."

By the time the game ended, she knew Dan would be gone. And her life would go on, exactly as she'd planned.

Which didn't mean it wouldn't hurt like hell whenever she thought of what might have been, had she or Dan been different.

Chapter Eleven

On a warm afternoon in June, Cassie Drennan stopped by the inn with her dad for a quick meeting about the wedding package she'd ordered for October. After almost a month of deliberation, Cassie had reached some big decisions that she wanted to discuss with Kinley, and her father had come along for the ride. Cassie confided to Kinley that her mom was out of town and her fiancé was in London, where they would be moving after the wedding, so she and her dad were spending the day together.

"We're having a nice dinner this evening and going out for a movie," she added, smiling happily at her father. "Daddy and I have always loved going to see action films together, haven't we?"

"We have," deep-voiced Paul Drennan agreed, and though he smiled, Kinley thought his jade eyes were a bit sad. She could only imagine how hard it must be for him to see his only daughter marrying and moving so far away. It was obvious that he and his ex had been quite young when Cassie was born. It was even more apparent that he adored his daughter, and that the feeling was mutual.

Kinley gave Cassie a copy of the agreement they'd signed, accepted a check from Paul and stood to open the office door for them. She recalled that the first time she'd met Cassie she'd thought it would be a pleasure working with her. That opinion was only reinforced by this meeting. She liked this family very much.

"Feel free to let me know if you want any changes," she said as she stood back to let them precede her into the entryway. "There's still plenty of time to make adjustments."

Which reminded her, of course, of the literally last-minute changes she'd made to Serena Sossaman-Thompson's wedding last month, which led her around to thinking of Dan, which made her heart hurt, as it always did when he crossed her mind.

She had become an expert at putting thoughts of him out of her mind, though they hovered constantly just around the periphery. She was confident that her smile never wavered when she added, "I'm sure it's going to be a beautiful wedding."

"I just hope the weather cooperates," Paul said over his shoulder as he moved to step out. "Cassie insisted on having an outdoor wedding, even though I warned her it could—oof."

Because he hadn't been watching where he was going, he had crashed straight into Bonnie, who'd been approaching from the desk. Both of them staggered back, though Paul quickly recovered and grabbed Bonnie's arms to steady her. "I'm so sorry. Totally my fault. Are you okay?"

"I'm fine." Her face beet-red, Bonnie smiled in embarrassment. "Oh. Mr. Drennan, isn't it?"

Cassie broke into peals of laughter. "Honestly, Daddy. Every time I bring you here, you barrel into this poor woman. I'm going to have to start leaving you at home before you break her arm or something."

Paul shot a repressive look at his amused daughter. "Cassie, it isn't funny. She could have been hurt."

"Actually, it is kind of funny," Bonnie said with an understanding smile at the younger woman. "I don't really walk into every client who comes in. Appearances to the contrary."

Kinley waved to the departing duo, then turned back to her sister, who had fallen into a chair at the table and covered her face with her hands. Smothering a grin, she asked, "Bon? You okay?"

"I'm mortified," Bonnie replied, her voice muffled. "Why is it that every time that man comes in I make a fool of myself?"

"He's only been here twice."

"And I've ploughed into him both times."

"Actually, I think it was his fault this time. He was looking one direction and walking another."

Bonnie dropped her hands. "He seems quite nice. Both of them do."

"They're great. It's going to be a lot of fun working with them. Her mother and stepdad are nice, too, from what I recall. Everyone seemed really pleasant together, which is always gratifying from a blended family."

"So there's not a stepmom?" Bonnie asked a bit too casually.

Kinley raised an eyebrow. She remembered now that Bonnie had seemed taken with Paul last time she'd literally run into him. It was an unlikely match, what with Paul being quite a bit older and the father of a young woman not many years younger than Bonnie—but who was she to criticize anyone for developing a fascination with a man who was all wrong for her? She just hoped her sister didn't end up crying into her pillow during unguarded moments in long, lonely nights.

"No," she said. "As far as I know, there's no stepmom."

Bonnie shrugged. "Just curious."

"Uh-huh. Sure."

"About that wedding shower we have booked for Sunday afternoon…"

An hour later, Kinley was out in the garden with her camera. She wanted a couple of new photos for the website, and the roses were truly beautiful now with the afternoon sun on them. She'd seen a couple of guests strolling along the paths earlier, but she seemed to be the only one out now. She snapped a few shots of the fountain, then moved to the future site of the Meditation Garden, where the yellow roses were in full bloom. Focusing tightly on one perfect blossom, she smiled in delight when a butterfly fluttered into the shot. Unless it had blurred, that should be a nice one. She was no professional photographer, but she enjoyed taking pictures.

She saw something move from the corner of her right eye. Glancing idly that way, she froze when she thought she saw the smiling woman in white again. Just standing there. Smiling at her.

Her fingers went nerveless, so that she almost dropped her camera, but when she whirled to get a better look, no one was there. Just a bush covered in tiny white blooms, the branches rustled by a breeze so faint Kinley didn't even feel it.

Shaking her head in self-disgust, she wondered if she would ever fully recover from those few crazy days in the spring. She was still jumping at shadows, still waking up sniffling, still battling an emptiness no amount of job success had been able to fill yet. A Dan-shaped hole in her heart, as she thought of it when she allowed herself to draw on dark humor for comfort. She'd get over it. Someday.

It hadn't been a failure, she assured herself as she had many times before. She couldn't fail if she'd never really tried...right?

Lifting the camera again, she focused on another flower, then a spreading Japanese maple. The camera still raised, she turned in search of another nice shot—only to find Dan Phelan's face framed in her viewfinder.

This time she did drop the camera. Had the strap not been looped around her wrist, it would have crashed to the pebbles at her feet, probably breaking the screen.

She closed her eyes for a moment, then looked again, but unlike the hazy image she'd thought she saw before, Dan was still there.

"You remember that question you asked me?" he said as if it hadn't been a full month since they'd last seen each other.

"I, uh..." She swallowed hard, working to recover her composure. "I'm sorry, what question?"

"You asked if I'm happy with the way I'm living."

She recalled that very clearly. It had concluded their conversation at the lookout tower, when everything had changed between them. When he'd decided so suddenly to leave.

Nervously smoothing her hands against her pants, she cleared her throat silently before saying, "Yes. I remember."

"I have an answer for you now," he said. He made no effort to move closer to her. He simply stood there, hands in the pockets of his jeans, his bright blue eyes leveled intently on her face.

"And?"

"And...no. I haven't been particularly happy."

"That's a shame," she murmured. "I thought you enjoyed your carefree life."

"I did, for several years. But it gets old, you know? Drifting. Looking for the next way to earn my parents' disapproval."

She heard the irony in his comment, and she knew he wasn't being literal. Despite his complicated relationship with his parents, Dan had made his choices for reasons of his own. He'd been following his dreams, looking for his own place in life, she realized abruptly. He'd expected his parents to disapprove, probably because they so often did.

"I know what it's like to spend your life trying to prove something," she told him quietly. "You've been trying to show everyone that you are your own man, free to make your own mistakes. I've been trying to convince everyone I don't make mistakes—not since my disaster of a marriage, anyway. Always in control, always on the job. That's me. And then Serena Sossaman pointed out that I'm turning into her mother. And I had to stop and ask myself if that was really what I wanted. You aren't the only one who's been rethinking your life during the past month."

Dan moved then, his hands dropping onto her shoulders, his expression stern. "You are nothing like Eva Sossaman," he told her flatly. "She means well, maybe, but she railroads over everyone to get what she wants. You don't do that. You care about what other people want. You do everything you can to make sure you provide it for them, which is why you're so successful here, and in your real-estate career. But maybe sometimes you forget to ask yourself what it is that *you* want."

She knew what she wanted right now. Wanted more than her next breath, in fact. And to her amazement, he was standing right in front of her.

"Do you remember the last thing you said to me before I left last month?" he asked huskily.

She moistened her lips. "I said I hoped you'd find what you were looking for."

"Yes." He smiled a little then, his fingers flexing on her shoulders in a light caress. "It took me a few weeks to realize that I'd already found it. Like an idiot, I got scared and walked away from what I'd been looking for all my life."

She felt her eyes widen. "Dan?"

"I know you think I'm not the serious and committed type. That I don't stick with anything very long. I know you don't know me well enough to fully trust me yet when I tell you I can make a commitment and stick with it. It took me a while to trust myself in that respect. I know you're much too practical and realistic to believe in love at first sight. That you believe in what you can touch and feel and prove with your ledger sheets. But if you'll give me a chance, I'll do my best to prove to you that I..."

With a smile, she reached up to lay her fingers against his mouth, stopping the flow of words in mid-sentence. "You don't have to prove anything to me, Dan," she murmured around a hard lump in her throat. "I've come to believe in a lot of things I can't explain during the past month. Love at first sight is only one of them."

His arms went around her, drawing her hard against him. His somber face lit with one of his amazing smiles, and his blue eyes were as bright as the sun when he looked down at her. "We'll take it slow from this point," he promised her. "All the time you need. I'll still have some traveling to do with my job for now—but I'll always come back to you."

"And I'll be very busy here with *my* job—but I'll always make time to welcome you back," she assured him, slipping her arms around his neck.

His lips moving against hers, he murmured, "I think this is going to work out very well."

"I have no doubt of it," she replied, then took his mouth with hers.

As the kiss deepened and heated, she had the strangest feeling that someone was watching them...and smiling.

Her bed was a tangled, rumpled mess, the covers half on, half off, pillows on the floor, a few items of clothing tossed across the headboard. Dan lay half across Kinley, sticky skin fused with hers as they breathed in ragged unison, trying to calm their pounding hearts and racing pulses.

They hadn't stayed at the inn long after he'd shown up so unexpectedly, only long enough to tell Bonnie he was back and that Kinley was taking the rest of the day off. Maybe tomorrow, as well.

Bonnie had heartily approved.

With an effort, Dan lifted his head, studying her flushed, damp face with visible satisfaction. "Now that," he said, "is what I call a welcome."

She laughed softly and nipped his shoulder, making him chuckle.

He kissed her lips, her cheek, then nuzzled into the curve of her shoulder. "Kinley?" he murmured.

Her eyes drifting closed as she ran her hands slowly down his sleek, warm back she responded, "Hmm?"

"That night in the woods. You saw her, didn't you?"

She froze, her eyes opening. "I—"

"You can deny it all you want, but I know you saw her, too."

"I saw…something," she admitted after a moment. "I'm not saying it was a ghost."

Dan grinned in satisfaction. "Neither am I. But I'm not saying it wasn't, either."

"Whatever it was, we'll keep it between us, shall we?" she asked with just a hint of pleading.

"Absolutely." He lowered his head again, stringing kisses from her ear to the curve of her shoulder. Then scooted down to explore the upper curve of her breast with his lips and teeth, his hand preceding him even lower.

"It doesn't matter, anyway," he said, his thumb circling lazily, making her mind spin in concert with the motion. "I don't need a ghost to tell me this is right. That it's going to last."

Her fingers sliding into his thick hair, Kinley arched into his touch, offering herself to him again. She didn't need a ghost, either, she thought happily. But it was nice to know the bride approved.

* * * * *

Join the Mills & Boon Book Club

Subscribe to **Cherish**™ today for 3, 6 or 12 months and you could **save over £40!**

We'll also treat you to these fabulous extras:

- FREE L'Occitane gift set worth £10

- FREE home delivery

- Rewards scheme, exclusive offers…and much more!

Subscribe now and save over £40
www.millsandboon.co.uk/subscribeme

Discover more romance at

www.millsandboon.co.uk

- ❤ WIN great prizes in our exclusive competitions

- ❤ BUY new titles before they hit the shops

- ❤ BROWSE new books and REVIEW your favourites

- ❤ SAVE on new books with the Mills & Boon® Bookclub™

- ❤ DISCOVER new authors

PLUS, to chat about your favourite reads, get the latest news and find special offers:

- 🔲 Find us on facebook.com/millsandboon

- ➤ Follow us on twitter.com/millsandboonuk

- ❤ Sign up to our newsletter at millsandboon.co.uk